A Murder in

Paradise

A Murder
in Paradise

A Logan & Cafferty
Mystery/Suspense Novel

Jean Henry Mead

Medallion Books
Glenrock, Wyoming

Published by Medallion Books and printed in the United States of America. No part of this book may be reproduced in any manner without the express permission of the publisher, with the exception of brief quotes used in critical articles and reviews. This is a work of fiction. The characters are figments of the author's imagination and bear no resemblance to persons living or dead.

Library of Congress cataloging pending

First edition published in November 2013

Book cover design by Bill Mead

ISBN: 978-1-931415-43-9

Other Medallion Books by Jean Henry Mead

A Village Shattered

Diary of Murder

Murder on the Interstate

Gray Wolf Mountain

Mystery of Spider Mountain

Ghost of Crimson Dawn

No Escape: A Wyoming Historical Novel

The Mystery Writers

Dedication:

**For my friends Judy Peterson
and Brenda Worrell Dinger**

Chapter One

The sun cast a deep orange glow across the small Texas lake. Seated near the shoreline, finishing their dinner on the resort patio, the two women watched as a duck repeatedly dived beneath the water. When he failed to surface, Sarah rose from the dining table and walked to the water's edge. Shading her eyes against the setting sun, she scanned the lake for some sign of the missing duck. When she failed to locate it, she walked several yards down the bank before turning back to yell, "Where'd it go? I don't see him anywhere."

Sighing, Dana left the remains of her meal to join her friend on the bank. When they were unable to spot the illusive fowl, Sarah decided that he'd made his last dive. Stooping to peer at a large clump of weeds, she said "There he is, in the bulrushes."

"What's that in his beak?"

Sarah removed her sandals to wade into the lake. "Looks like a piece of silk." Halting her forward motion, she shrieked, "Oh, no, there's an arm attached."

As she approached, a large, red-headed duck with

light feathers seemed to run on the water before lifting into the sky. A piece of bright blue cloth still dangled from his beak.

Dana removed her own sandals to wade in after her friend, the water chilling her knees. Parting the weeds several yards from shore, she gasped when she discovered a woman face up in the water, her long red hair floating behind her like rosy tentacles. Dressed in skimpy denim shorts and a torn silk blouse, she didn't appear to be breathing when Dana gripped her nearest wrist to find a pulse.

"We've got to get her ashore." Dana grabbed the woman's tanned bare feet, telling Sarah to call 911.

A small crowd gathered when they reached the bank where two men helped to lift the woman ashore. Placing her on the golf course turf, one of them immediately began CPR.

Both women were pelted with questions as soon as Sarah's call ended. But before they could answer, a woman said, "It's Varina Zagori."

Dana heard another woman grumble behind her. "Someone must have killed her."

When she turned to ask why, their fellow RVers had already started back toward the nearest motorhome.

Puzzled, Dana asked, "When will the ambulance arrive?"

"I was told twenty minutes. We're quite a ways from town."

"Why does this always happen? We can't even vacation without a body turning up."

Sarah shook her head. "I saw that woman this morning just after you backed the motorhome onto our lot. She and another golfer were putting on the green behind us and I guess they didn't realize I could hear them."

"What did they say?"

"They paused their game to stare at us before that one"—she indicated the woman on the ground—"said something strange about us."

"What did we do, back over one of her golf balls?"

"No, Dana. She laughed at the way were dressed and said we must be traveling dikes."

"Why would she say something like that?" Dana realized she would have to lower her voice when people turned to stare. Taking Sarah's arm, she led her some distance from the crowd as a security golf cart raced up with two people aboard. Jumping out, they ran to where the victim lay. Dana doubted the woman would survive, despite everyone's efforts to save her.

As they watched the assembled emergency team at work, Dana asked in a quiet voice, "What's this about us being—?"

"I shouldn't have told you."

"I'm glad you did. It's a clue to the woman's character if she had a habit of making snap judgments about people she didn't know." Dana ground her teeth. "You know how I feel about nasty gossips, especially those who make racial and homophobic slurs."

"I agree. They need to get a life." Sarah lowered herself to the grass. "But why would someone stop her golf game to say something like that?"

"Maybe it's our height difference."

Sarah smiled. "Our Sew and So club members *did* call us Mutt and Jeff."

"But they said it affectionately. I don't think the Zagori woman was being nice. She probably made nasty remarks about everyone she saw."

"At least the golfer with her said her remark was uncalled for."

"That woman behind us could have been right. The victim might have made someone so mad that he killed her."

"Then again, she might have accidentally drowned."

"Face up in the water? I doubt it."

An ambulance's wail could be heard in the distance, prompting onlookers to move away from those still working on the victim. From the expressions on their faces, it seemed a lost cause.

Before the ambulance arrived, a small white dog sniffed his way to the body, then turned and made his way across the golf course. Was it the victim's dog? If so, he didn't seem to be mourning his owner.

Dana remembered seeing a ring on the victim's left hand. Where was her husband? He should have been home from work by now, if he wasn't retired or there on vacation. Maybe *he* was responsible for her death. Spouses were always prime suspects, but Dana had a feeling there was much more involved than a domestic squabble. From the brief comments she'd heard earlier, Varina Zagori wasn't a popular resident of the RV resort.

A patrol car screeched to a halt nearby, closely followed by an ambulance. She and Sarah waited, knowing the sheriff or his deputy would want to question them. After a brief inspection of the body, the sheriff approached them and they were led to a picnic table for questioning.

A tall, ruggedly handsome man introduced himself as Sheriff Steve Brandson. He vaguely reminded Dana of her amorous friend, Sheriff Walter Grayson, although he was younger and more than a few pounds slimmer.

He wasn't smiling when he asked, "Are you the two women who found the body?"

Sarah said they were. "We seem to be murder magnets. No matter where we go, we manage to find a body."

Dana nudged her friend under the picnic table. When she flinched, Dana said, "We've had the unfortunate experience of becoming involved in a number of murder investigations."

She would have given the sheriff Walter's cell number for reference but didn't want her suitor to know where they were. She knew he would track them down eventually, but hoped for some quiet time before he persuaded her to marry him.

"Please elaborate." The sheriff impatiently tapped his pad with a pen.

With Sarah's help, she managed to fill him in on all the previous murder cases they'd become involved in. When he frowned while taking notes, Dana said, "We seemed to be cursed—always in the wrong place when a body turns up. I'm sure you understand."

His expression said he didn't. "This is no joking matter, ma'am. The two of you need to come to my office as soon as I finish my preliminary investigation."

"But we just arrived from Wyoming, Sheriff." Sarah's face crumpled. "We didn't even know the victim."

"Two older women traveling in an RV discovering bodies is mighty unusual, if you ask me."

At least he didn't say old women. Sarah's piteous expression evolved into a smile. She must feel flattered that they hadn't been referred to as a couple of demented seniors. Then again, maybe she was thinking of the film, "Arsenic and Old Lace."

The coroner's van pulled in behind the ambulance as the sheriff wrote down their names, ages and other vital information.

He told them he would be taking them into town for further questioning. Dana dreaded the trip in the back of a patrol car. She hoped they weren't considered persons of interest as she watched the sheriff talk to the EMTs, who were loading their equipment into the ambulance. They were taking their time, their siren silent when they left the area.

Another vehicle arrived, which Dana assumed was the forensics team. Deputies were also cordoning off the area with yellow crime tape. How strange that so many law enforcement departments had arrived so soon for a suspected drowning.

Dana remarked how beautiful the resort was as they were herded to the patrol car. "Not the place you'd expect to find a body."

"An RVer's paradise," a deputy replied. "I wish I could afford a nice rig and an RV lot by one of the lakes. You people don't know how lucky you are."

Lucky? In many ways they were. They were able to travel wherever they pleased, thanks to the generous inheritance Dana had received from her deceased sister, Georgi. She bit her lip, willing away the painful memory of her sister's body in the crematorium after she was murdered.

Chapter Two

They reached the sheriff's office some twenty minutes later. Escorted inside, they were told to wait in an anteroom, where they sat for nearly half an hour. Sarah fidgeted, bemoaning the fact that they hadn't prepared dinner in their motorhome instead of dining at the lakeside restaurant.

"Probably because we were supposed to find the body."

"Why us, Dana? Why are we always tripping over murder victims?"

Dana glanced briefly at the ceiling. "Maybe it's our calling. They say everyone comes to earth for a reason."

"Who are *they*? I'd like to know who's been setting us up." Sarah left her chair to pace the small room furnished with four chairs.

Dana smiled. "You enjoy the challenge of solving murders as much as I do, and I don't think this case will be too difficult to solve. First of all, the woman is obviously well known—"

"And second, she's not well liked," Sarah finished

for her. "Probably for good reason."

"Right. All we have to do is visit with the other RVers and listen to what they have to say. The death's going to be a major topic of conversation around here for quite some time."

"This case is different. Have you noticed the license plates from around the country? I also saw names in the guest book from foreign countries. And some million dollar motorhomes."

The door opened and a deputy beckoned them into another room. The sheriff was seated behind his massive desk wearing the same frown he'd displayed earlier.

"Ladies, I'm investigating four murders that have taken place within the county during the past five weeks. The Zagori woman may be number five. So I want to know exactly what happened and why you waded in the lake."

Smoothing her damp capris, Sarah said, "We saw this unusual looking duck diving in the water and I wondered if it was a canvasback."

The sheriff leaned forward in his chair, his elbow's resting on his desk. "A what?"

"You're not a duck hunter, are you?"

"No, ma'am, I don't have the time."

Her short curly blond hair bobbed as she spoke. "My husband Terry was a duck hunter who educated me about water fowl. There are very few ducks that dive underwater."

His expression said *get on with it.*

"I was concerned when the drake didn't resurface. So I went to investigate."

When they had finished telling him all they knew, he said they were free to leave the office, although not the county. Sarah offered their investigative skills and was promptly turned down.

"I have enough murders to investigate. If a killer's on the loose, I don't wanna find any more victims, especially witnesses."

Dana assured him they would be careful. "We'll let you know if we hear anything that will help your investigation."

He nodded, allowing a small grin. Punching a button on his desk phone, he told a deputy to drive them back to Paradise Acres. Dana knew he would be grateful for any useful leads they could uncover, although he didn't encourage them.

During the ride back to the RV resort, she made a mental note to stock up on wine and cheese to entertain their neighbors. RVers were usually a friendly group and were probably more candid with a fellow traveler than they would be with law enforcement. Checking her watch, she noted the time. A trip to the market for supplies was in order the following day.

They decided to take a walking tour of the resort after returning from shopping. Few neighbors were out of doors and those that were merely nodded when Sarah greeted them. Not the friendly RVers they'd expected. Word was out that a murder had been committed in Paradise Acres.

"We should have brought Jenny along," Dana said. "Dog owners are always willing to talk about their pooches."

Sarah sighed. "It's a long walk to the dog park from here. Jenny can ride in the back of the golf cart."

"We won't be able to talk to people if we ride."

"You're right. We need the exercise as much as she

does. Let's free her from the motorhome. I'm sure she's tired of watching the pet channel."

When they returned, Jenny happily accepted her leash and they set off for the dog park, expecting to meet someone willing to talk along the way. But the park was surprisingly quiet. Everyone seemed to be in hiding, so maybe they should rethink their walk. When they reached the dog park, they found it deserted.

Sarah sat on a bench to rest. "Wrong time of day. We should have waited until late this afternoon when most dogs do their business."

Dana closed the gate and unleashed the dog. Jenny briefly sniffed her new territory before bounding about the enclosure as though a small child at play.

"The older she gets," Sarah observed, "the more she resembles a wolf."

"Maybe that's because she *is* a wolf, captured as a pup and raised as a dog."

Sarah grimaced. "I'm aware of Jenny's background, and it makes me wonder if that's why no one wants to talk to us. They could be afraid of Jenny."

"You could be right. We'd better take her back to the motorhome." Reaching to pet their wolf dog, Dana reattached the leash.

When they reached home, Dana filled a lazy susan with cheeses and crackers while Sarah walked next door to invite the neighbors over. It wasn't long before a middle aged couple made their way to the patio beside their motorhome. The plump, pleasant woman who resembled Sarah was all smiles. Wearing flip flops and a knee length summer shift, she introduced her husband, a tall, balding man with irregular eyebrows. He seemed more reserved and allowed his wife to do the talking.

Dana noticed that his knobby knees were trembling

slightly beneath his cargo shorts. Why was he nervous? Did he know something about Varina Zagori's death or had his wife dragged him over against his will?

Mona and Hubert helped themselves to the wine and cheese as though they hadn't eaten that day. With their mouths full of chips, her guests only replied to casual questions with hearty nods.

"I noticed your Ohio license plate," Sarah said. "Have you been here long?"

Mona held up two fingers as she wiped her mouth with the back of her other hand. Her husband nodded his agreement. "Two weeks," he said, finishing off the jalapeno dip.

Dana decided the time was right, "I don't suppose you've met a woman named Varina Zagori."

"Who?"

"The woman who was murdered here yesterday?"

Mona's face took on an ashen color and Dana feared she would lose what she had eaten. Without asking for details, Hubert wasted no time taking his wife's arm and steering her back to their fifth wheel trailer. It wasn't long before they heard the trailer's slide-outs slide in and the roar of their pickup's engine.

"Looks like they're leaving, Dana."

"They must not have heard that this place is on lockdown."

"We need to be a little more subtle next time. Let people bring up the subject themselves."

"I wonder if Mona and Hubert will be suspects when the sheriff discovers they're trying to leave."

Dana began to clear away the remains of their failed wine and cheese party. "I'm not surprised that the sheriff has this place on lockdown. It *is* a gated community."

"He's probably got a deputy or two outside the park

waiting for people leaving without permission. Then he'll run an NCIC on them. I'm sure Mona and Hubert will ask directions to the nearest RV park."

"Sheriff Brandson is probably running background checks on everyone. Let's take another walk around the park to see if anyone's willing to talk."

"There hasn't been any official word yet issued that it *was* murder, Dana. Most people are probably wondering why they can't leave the resort."

"The Zagori woman's blouse was ripped and she might have drowned. That has murder imprinted all over it."

"You're right, but let's not call it that when we talk to the neighbors. We don't want to cause a mass exodus."

After the chips and dips were put away, they sat to discuss their strategy. Deciding that it was too soon after the woman's death to plan a get acquainted party for the neighbors, they decided to meet their fellow travelers at the resort chapel. Church services were scheduled for the following day.

<><><>

Next morning when they arrived at the small chapel, they found the parking lot filled with golf carts, some of them parked four carts deep.

During the service, Varina Zagori was eulogized and a hymn sung in her honor. No one seemed to be crying or unduly upset, which surprised them both. What had the woman done to turn everyone against her? Was it simply her nasty tongue?

On their way to the chapel's entrance, an attractive, dark haired man probably in his early fifties stood alone, shaking hands with those who were leaving the service. Dana assumed he was the victim's husband.

His cheerless blue eyes told her he was upset by his wife's death, but not unduly so. She hoped to get a chance to talk to him.

The parking lot was filled with people, some ready to leave. Others stood stony-faced as though waiting for something to happen. Dana and Sarah waited with them, attempting to strike up conversations, but no one seemed willing to talk. Perhaps the reason for their standoffishness was that the two of them were strangers. After long, frustrating moments, they decided to return to the chapel to offer their condolences.

"I wonder if this was meant to be a memorial service," Sarah whispered. "Maybe the body's going to be cremated."

"I think it's too soon. They'll probably wait for an autopsy to determine the cause of death." She took Sarah's arm and led her back into the chapel where the grieving man stood, talking to the minister. His tall, angular body was stooped as he listened to the much shorter cleric. Standing nearby, they pretended to engage in quiet conversation as they listened to what the two men had to say.

"Jerome, I know this is difficult," the minister said, "but the Lord will ease your pain. You must keep the faith."

"We were in the process of filing for divorce. My wife was in love with someone else."

The minister looked about as though to determine whether anyone was listening. When he noticed Dana and Sarah standing nearby, he gripped the man's arm and led him into another room, quietly closing the door."

Sarah whispered, "A motive for murder."

"Do you really think Varina's husband would admit his guilt in public, so soon after her death?"

"If he has a guilt complex, he might. And he knows the preacher won't squeal on him."

"You've been watching too many police shows, Sarah. You're beginning to sound like a member of the mob."

Sarah made a face. "I wonder who Varina was in love with. Maybe they had a lover's spat."

"Once we get to know the people here, I'm sure they'll tell us who he is. It's a large resort but a small community where they all know each other's business."

"You're right. The Zagoris must live here, at least part time, or there wouldn't have been so many people at the service."

"Maybe they're as curious as we are, unless murders are commonplace, which is doubtful in such an isolated area."

They walked back into the parking lot, which had emptied except for a lingering man. Tall and stocky with a bulbous nose, he walked over to appraise them.

"You're new here, aren't you? Renters or property owners?"

Dana hesitated. "Renters for the time being. We were considering buying a lot until—"

He smiled. "Oh, don't let Varina's death change your mind about buying one of our beautiful lots. My golf cart's right here. Why don't I show you around?"

"We've been around," Sarah told him, "and this is *not* a friendly place."

The man appeared surprised. "Of course it is. Everyone's still in shock because Varina has passed. She must have had a heart attack and fallen in the lake and drowned."

"Do you really believe that's what happened?"

He nodded and pulled business cards from his pocket. Handing one to each of them, he introduced himself as Paul Gates, the local realtor.

"I'm Dana Logan and this is my friend Sarah Cafferty. We're here on vacation and didn't expect to find a body in the lake."

"Oh, so you're the ones who discovered her."

Sarah nodded "I don't think falling in the lake would have ripped the woman's blouse."

Gates chewed his lip for a moment before he said, "There's nothing like a little intrigue to make life interesting."

"Speaking of intrigue," Sarah said. "We understand the Zagori woman was having an affair."

Gates choked as though he had swallowed his tie. "Where'd you hear that?"

"Local gossip."

"Well, this *is* a little Peyton Place but I never would have suspected that Varina—Missus Zagori—was having an affair."

"Then why did the other women dislike her?"

Gates hesitated. "She was an attractive woman and I'm sure others were jealous of her."

"Jealous enough to kill her?"

"Certainly not. We don't have those kinds of people staying in our resort."

"Some wealthy people have committed homicide."

"That may be true." He stooped in a slight bow, swinging his arm toward his four-seated golf cart. "Our chariot awaits, ladies. Allow me to give you the grand tour of Paradise Acres."

The women exchanged glances and decided to take him up on his offer.

Chapter Three

Dana had to admit that the resort was impressive. Expensive motorhomes and fifth wheel trailers were parked in large, well groomed lots that were adorned with a variety of trees and flowers. Luscious green grass surrounded the RVs, leading to the golf course, which meandered through the maze of recreational vehicles.

Most lots had outdoor kitchens, a variety of canopies and dining areas. Some sported small garages or adobe casitas which resembled miniature houses. Their host stopped to point out the amenities of each lot for sale until they grew tired of the grand tour. He had only one thing on his mind and that was sales.

When he finally dropped them off at their lot, Dana said she was interested in buying but wanted to know more about the resort. She beckoned him to their patio, and offered him a glass of wine. Once he was seated with a goblet of cabernet sauvignon in hand, they casually asked about the inhabitants of the park as well as the various activities.

Smiling broadly and obviously preparing for a sale,

he said, "This is the friendliest place on the planet. When someone's sick or has a problem, the neighbor's all rush to help."

Sarah smiled. "Friendly enough for a mercy killing?"

Gates set his glass down so hard on the table that Dana was afraid it would break. "I wish you ladies would stop referring to Varina's death as murder. The poor woman was in ill health and must have fainted before she fell in the lake."

Sarah set her own glass down more gently. "That doesn't explain her torn blouse."

"As you can see, we have plenty of water fowl here. Depending on how long Varina was in the water, the ducks or geese could have mistaken her clothing for food."

Sarah snorted. "That seems a bit farfetched, don't you think?"

Gates glanced at his watch before pushing back his chair. The scraping sound on concrete made Dana cringe. "It's late and I'm sure dinner's waiting. I'll check back tomorrow to see which lot you prefer." He hurried to his golf cart without another word.

When the cart disappeared, Dana said, "What do you make of that?"

"He definitely knows something. He may even be the man Varina Zagori was having an affair with."

"I agree. If he shows up here tomorrow, he's either desperate for a sale, or braver than I give him credit for."

"Brave, Dana? Why?"

"He was nervous as an expectant father in a delivery room. He's not going to tell us more about the murdered woman."

"I thought we weren't referring to her as the murder victim until the autopsy report."

"Oh, she was murdered all right."

"How can you be sure?"

Dana leaned forward and lowered her voice. "She wasn't wearing a bra and her shorts were unzipped. She didn't have anything under them."

"Not even a thong?" Sarah appeared shocked. "Why didn't I notice that?"

"Probably because you were more interested in the duck."

Sarah hung her head, muttering to herself. "I'd never seen a diving canvasback before."

Dana patted her shoulder. "It's okay. At least one of us was observant. It's your turn next time."

Sarah smiled. "That's what I love you about you, Dana. You can put people down and make them feel good about it?"

"Well, at least I'm good at something."

"And I'm not?"

"Of course you are, Sarah. You have a way of putting people at ease. And taking down their guard. That's a trait I wish I had."

"We're a good team. Together we'll solve this murder like we did all the others."

"I wish I had your confidence, my friend. I have a feeling this case is going to be like peeling an artichoke, one bud at a time."

"Surely the sheriff knows that Varina Zagori was murdered."

"He knows but he doesn't want to cause a panic among the resort residents."

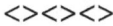

Next morning at dawn, Dana was awakened by a sharp bark. Someone must have knocked at the motorhome door. Hurrying into her robe and slippers, she heard Sarah snore from the adjacent bunk. She could sleep through a hurricane.

When Dana opened the door, no one was in sight, but Jenny still had her teeth bared. What in the world was going on? She reached to pet the dog and felt hair standing on her back as stiff as a bristle brush. Something must have frightened the dog. Opening the blinds on the opposite side of the coach, she peered out into the semi-darkness. Storm clouds threatened rain and a possible thunderstorm. They should have watched the evening news before retiring the previous night.

Jenny seemed to relax as she curled at Dana's feet. Why would someone knock that early when most people were still asleep? Unless it was an emergency.

Sarah padded into the kitchen half an hour later to find Dana sitting at the breakfast nook sipping green tea.

"You missed the excitement."

Sarah yawned and plopped down opposite her. "What excitement? Did they find another body?"

"I hope not, but something made Jenny bark this morning."

"I thought I dreamed it, Dana. We were swimming in the lake when a flock of drakes attacked and tried to rip off our clothes."

Dana laughed. "Wishful thinking?"

"Wrong kind of drakes, but it got me to thinking about what the realtor said about ducks ripping the Zagori woman's blouse."

"Do you think that's possible?"

Sarah shook her head. "Anything's possible, but no, I don't think that's what happened. I'll bet she was killed by a jealous husband. Or an angry lover."

"Makes sense to me. But there are a lot of men in this resort who could have killed her."

"I don't think it was Gates."

"Why?"

"Varina was an attractive woman." Sarah left the nook to make herself a cup of tea. "And Gates is rather homely."

"Some women prefer men they don't have to worry about."

"That's true, but her husband is a nice looking man. Why would she choose someone—?"

"Looks aren't everything. Maybe the boyfriend was nicer or"—

"Better in bed?"

"Maybe. I think we need to join a social club here where we can listen in on gossip, as much as I hate it. The Zagori woman's death has got to be the main topic of conversation."

"Which club shall we join, Dana? Cards, sewing, knitting—?"

"I saw a photography group listed in the brochure."

"Sounds like fun. They must go on picture taking outings."

"Someone might have snapped a picture of the victim and her boyfriend." Dana slid from the breakfast nook and made her way to the cupboard. "Let's go sign up for the photography club."

Jenny raised her head and barked as though to say *you're not leaving me behind again.*

Sarah thought she must be hungry and filled her dish with food. "I'm afraid the photography club won't allow you to attend, Jenny. On second thought, I'll bet they've never seen a wolf dog. Think of all the pictures they'll snap of you, my pet."

Jenny leaned her head to one side and Dana could

have sworn the dog smiled. "Pictures later, our doggie friend. We need to get dressed and sign up at the office."

Half an hour later, they were standing in line at the counter, listening to a quarrelsome old man debate his electric bill with the receptionist. By the time the discussion was over, Sarah was leaning with eyes closed against the wall. Dana could have sworn she had fallen asleep on her feet.

The dark haired, fortyish man behind the counter was abrupt and obviously still annoyed by his last encounter. When Dana told him what they had in mind, he sighed.

"Time for my break but we'll make this quick." Holding up his hand for patience, he strode into another room.

Sarah yawned as she leaned over the counter to pick up a greeting card. Before Dana could protest, she opened the card and read, "All my love, Varina."

Dana demanded that she place it exactly where she found it. A moment later the man returned.

"Ladies, you're in luck. There are two openings left in the photography club." He handed them each a form to fill out before they left.

"Was Varina Zagori a member of the club?" Sarah asked.

A dark scowl crept across his handsome face. "As a matter of fact she was. Why do you ask?"

Sarah lowered her eyes to the counter. "She was so pretty that I thought she might have been the club's model. You know, like student artists have."

"I don't think so." He sounded angry. "I'm the office manager. I'm filling in for my receptionist who's off sick today... Leave your forms on the counter after you fill them out. Now, excuse me." He abruptly left the room with the card in hand.

When they were sure he was out of earshot, Sarah whispered, "Another suspect."

"I was thinking the same thing. I wonder why that card was there."

"Sentimental reasons, Dana. If he were in love with Varina, he wouldn't want to destroy the card."

"But why take a chance that someone would see it?"

"He's wearing a wedding ring. He probably kept the card here at the office so his wife wouldn't find it."

"We need to check out the resort's roster to learn his name."

"This is going to be a tedious investigation. Can you imagine how many people work in this place?"

"Quite a few, and don't forget the groundskeepers. There must be at least twenty of them driving around in golf carts."

Dana led the way back to their own golf cart and they returned to the motorhome. It didn't take them long to discover how disgruntled Jenny had become in their absence. Every tissue box had been emptied, the contents briefly chewed and scattered throughout the coach. Pillows had also been chewed and shredded along with Sarah's lace doily collection. Everything had to be tossed in the trash.

"Bad dog," Sarah scolded, although her heart obviously wasn't in it. Poor Jenny was lonely and they needed to take her for a walk. After they cleaned up the mess, they hooked the leash to her collar and left the RV.

Dana thought it might be a good idea to return to the scene of the murder. They had seen someone with a dog in tow earlier at the outdoor restaurant, so they stopped for a cup of coffee. Jenny patiently waited at Sarah's feet as they discussed in low tones what they had learned so far.

First on their list was the victim's husband, next the aggressive realtor, and last the office manager. Sarah suggested a jealous wife. "What if the manager's wife found out about his affair?"

Dana said, "When does the photography club meet? We need more input before we start investigating."

Sarah opened her purse and retrieved the schedule. "Looks like we're in luck. The club meets tomorrow morning at nine."

Jenny growled and bared her teeth when a man passed near their table. The middle aged Latino, of average height and weight, was casually dressed in a tee shirt and khakis. He grinned at them beneath a neat pencil mustache.

"Enjoying your coffee, ladies?" He spoke with a distinct accent.

Sarah nodded. "Why don't you join us?"

Dana gasped when her friend pushed back a chair. The man hesitated when he heard Jenny growl.

"I don't think your dog likes me," he said, backing away.

"No problem. I'll tie her to the tree near the lake."

What was Sarah up to and why was she inviting this stranger to sit with them? She soon learned why. When her friend returned to the table, she smiled at the man now seated next to her.

"Are you one of the resort residents?" she asked.

"No, ma'am. I'm one of the groundskeepers. I wish I could afford to live here. This is my day off and I stopped in to talk to my supervisor."

Dana noticed he wasn't wearing a ring as Sarah leaned in closer.

"You must know what happens here on a daily basis."

He nodded, apparently uncomfortable with Sarah's

questions.

"Did you know the woman pulled from the lake?"

"Si. She was sometimes nice to me."

"Sometimes?"

"When she wanted me to do something."

"Did you ever see her with a man not her husband?"

He fidgeted in his chair and looked to Dana as if for help.

Dana assured him they were private investigators. But she didn't tell him how private.

He looked from one to the other before saying, "I saw her talking to a lot of men but I don't know if"—he hesitated—"there was anything going on between them."

"Did anyone you know hate her?"

He laughed. "I'm sure a lot of women didn't like her because she flirted a lot and was always hugging their husbands."

"Anyone in particular?"

"Not my business, ladies. I don't spy on people. I just help keep this place looking nice."

"We admire that in a man, don't we, Dana?"

As though that were his cue, he left the table and walked away.

Dana grumbled, "This is getting to be a habit."

"Men making a getaway?"

"No wonder the poor man left. You practically sat in his lap."

Sarah laughed. "He *was* kind of cute."

"You're impossible."

Her pudgy friend left her chair so quickly that it nearly capsized. "I'll go untie Jenny and we can walk around the lake."

Dana sighed as she rose to follow. She hoped that photography club members would talk about the

Zagori woman's death. Sarah was beckoning to her. She seemed anxious to walk the shoreline looking for clues. Stopping opposite the weeds where the body had been found, she noticed Jenny straining at the leash, nearly pulling Sarah into the lake. Dana didn't think wolves were fond of water, but Jenny already had her feet wet.

"What she's after, Sarah?"

Sarah kicked off her sandals and waded into the water. Stooping to retrieve a small object, she lifted it for Dana to see.

"Looks like a folded note. You know how Jenny likes chewing paper." Handing the leash to Dana, she carefully unfolded the soggy missive. "The writing's so blurred, I can't make it out, but by the narrow, distinctive slant, it looks like a woman's writing."

"We'd better turn this over to the sheriff to analyze. I wonder why his deputies didn't find it."

"Maybe it just floated free of the weeds."

Sarah rolled her capris over her knees and waded further into the lake. "I'm going over to the place where we found the body. There might be more clues that the police didn't find."

"Not likely. Be careful of water snakes."

"I might get lucky and have a close up look at a diving duck. There might even be a nest of eggs in the weeds."

"You're looking for clues, not ducks."

Sarah smiled and dismissed her as she disappeared into the weeds. Nearly five minutes later, Dana called to her friend. What in the world was she doing in there? Suddenly frightened, she found a bush to loop the leash around, telling Jenny to stay. Then, removing her shoes, she waded in after Sarah. She found her parting weeds to get a better look at something in the water.

"You scared me to death. What are you doing?"

"I saw something small and orange in the mud, but I can't quite reach it."

"It might not have anything to do with the murder, Sarah."

"But it might. My arms are too short. Why don't you try reaching for it?

Dana stared at her for a moment, then resigned herself to digging in the mud. The manicure she'd had prior to their trip was in bad need of repair, so she plunged in her right arm and groped among the weeds. She felt something crawling on her hand and shrieked. Waving fingers in the air, she heard Sarah laugh.

"It's just a little water bug, Dana. They don't bite."

"Looks like a roach to me." Hiking up her walking shorts, she headed for the bank. "Jenny and I are going home. You can weed dive as long as you like."

She heard Sarah splashing behind her. "Tomorrow we'll wear rubber gloves."

A wet suit's more like it, Dana thought, as she untied Jenny and offered a hand to Sarah. There had to be an easier way.

Chapter Four

The next morning they cleaned their digital cameras and stuffed long lenses in their camera bags. Anticipating a field trip, they wore tee shirts, hiking boots and jeans. Their bush hats were stowed in the golf cart along with their camera equipment. When they arrived at the clubhouse, the other members had already gone inside. Standing at the entrance, Dana noticed that she and Sarah were objects of amusement.

"Looks like we're underdressed," Sarah whispered. "They all look as though they're attending a Tupperware party."

"Let's go home and change."

When they returned to the clubhouse, a speaker was extolling the virtues of using the automatic camera function, so they quietly seated themselves in the back of the room. Disappointed, Dana realized this was a beginner's group—women who probably knew little or nothing about photography. She thought she heard Sarah snoring halfway through the lecture.

When the photographer left the platform, everyone

headed for the refreshments table. Sarah was first in line and wasted no time grabbing a handful of cookies, washing them down with a cup of coffee. Dana was more interested in the conversation taking place behind her.

"That poor man," one of them said. "All alone now that his wife's gone. I think I'll invite him to dinner."

"Good idea, Phyllis. I'll bake one of my blueberry pies."

There was a pause before Phyllis said, "I meant just the two of us, Leona. We don't want to overwhelm him."

Dana smiled, wondering how many widows lived in the resort, besides herself and Sarah.

"What do you think caused Varina's death?"

"I heard it had something to do with drugs."

"You think she overdosed on a prescription?"

"That happens to some of us with poor memories."

Dana curbed the urge to turn around to see who was talking, but they said nothing more. Taking a cup of coffee, she joined Sarah at a small table near the entrance. "Heard anything interesting?"

Sarah was too busy picking cookie crumbs from her napkin. She simply shook her head.

"We're here to eavesdrop, *not* gain weight."

A foursome sat down at the next table and all heads turned to appraise them. Dana smiled and introduced herself and Sarah as new members.

"Aren't you the ones who found the body?" a stout, blonde woman asked.

"I'm afraid so. It was horrifying."

A petite, dark-haired younger woman groaned. "Did you know Varina?" When Dana admitted they didn't, she said, "Lucky you."

Dana waited for an explanation, although none was forthcoming. Rising from her seat, she asked to join them. When they had exchanged pleasantries and places of origin, a petite, gray-haired woman said, "We heard you were taken to the sheriff's office for questioning. Did they tell you anything?"

"Nothing," Sarah said. "We were hoping someone could tell us why Varina died."

Their grunts of displeasure sounded like a chorus of aging bears. "You had to know the woman," one of them said. "She had no morals and never had a good thing to say about anyone."

Dana sighed. "Too bad she was so pessimistic."

"Not only that. She thought she was better than everyone."

"God's gift to men," the brunette said.

"So you think she was murdered?"

Their fellow club members eyed one another before nodding yes.

"Who?" Sarah demanded, wiping cookie dust from her chin.

"It could have been anyone. She only had one friend, other than certain men in the resort."

"Married men?" Sarah prompted.

"Some of them."

Sarah said, "The sheriff asked us to call him with any new evidence we might turn up."

"You're kidding," the blonde said. "Why you two?"

Sarah told them about the other murder cases they'd helped to solve. Those at the table listened intently, apparently enthralled. When Dana looked up, their table was surrounded with other club members. Nudging Sarah, she warned them to keep the information to themselves. "We're in space six nineteen, if you hear anything that might help solve the case."

"By the way, when are we planning a field trip?" Sarah asked.

"Field trip?" several women said. "We don't take

field trips."

Dana groaned. "That's what photography clubs do."

"That would be fun," someone said. "Let's plan an overnight trip to Dallas."

Sarah laughed. "That's not the kind of wildlife photography we had in mind. And we're not allowed to leave the county."

Dana sat staring at club members as they filed from the clubhouse. They had accomplished little besides placing fresh targets on their backs. She had a feeling the killer might have been present. Or had she become paranoid?

Sarah stood and slid her chair under the table. "Let's go before Jenny makes another mess. Too bad we can't leave her outside the motorhome. If she barks while we're gone, we'll be asked to leave the resort."

"We've been ordered to stay in the county, Sarah, but I don't think the sheriff can demand that the resort owners allow us to stay. I'm sure they wouldn't care if we were caught crossing the county line in search of another RV park."

"Then let's dig in our heels and solve the murder."

"The word's out. You know all those club members can't keep a secret. We'll have to be careful. I wonder what the concealed gun carry laws are here in Texas."

Sarah shrugged. "If we were home in Wyoming, you wouldn't need a gun permit."

"I almost wish we'd never left home."

"If wishes were horses, beggars would ride."

"Yes, Sarah, and golfers would all hit holes in one."

"Varina Zagori played golf. Maybe we should play a few rounds to get to know the other golfers."

"That would really place targets on our backs."

Sarah cringed. "As badly as we play, they'd probably laugh us off the course."

"I think our clubs are best left in the RV's storage compartment."

"We'd better stash a couple of irons in the motorhome for protection, just in case."

"Good thinking, Sherlock. Tomorrow, I'll apply for a Texas concealed carry permit."

<><><>

"I'm glad I still had my old Wyoming gun permit in my wallet," Dana said as they left the courthouse. "I almost threw it away when the no-permit carry law was passed."

"They have some strange laws here, making you wear your permit and picture on your belt."

"I don't mind. At least we have some protection in case the killer wants to add more notches to his belt."

Sarah said she felt safer with Dana carrying, but that it might cause problems with other RVers, especially those from other states. She reminded her of the growing number of firearms opponents across the country, although she doubted there were many in Texas or Wyoming.

"More than eight times as many murders are committed with knives and other weapons than guns, and this killer seems to prefer golf balls and water."

They arrived back at the resort twenty minutes later, surprised to find a crowd gathered outside the main clubhouse. Dana wasn't able to find a parking place large enough for the Jeep, so they drove back to the motorhome to check on Jenny before climbing in the golf cart. Dana drove around the resort several times before she found a parking space a block away from the clubhouse.

The crowd seemed to have grown larger. Standing

quietly at the back of the assemblage, they strained to hear what the sheriff's deputy was saying from the landing. Dana caught the words "head injury."

A tall man with a heavy paunch yelled, "What kind of head injury?"

The young deputy folded arms across his chest before answering. "The forensics lab confirmed that it was made by a small object the size of a golf ball."

Sarah gasped. "The killer's a golfer."

Someone wearing a baseball cap asked, "Could it have been an accident?"

The deputy twisted his mouth in thought. "Anything's possible."

Everyone turned to look at those around them. Not an accident, Dana thought. *Not the way Varina Zagori was dressed. Or undressed.*

A petite woman standing ahead of Sarah called, "Do you think she was hit by a stray ball and fell in the lake?"

"Not my call," the deputy replied. "But I want all you golfers to come into the clubhouse and register with my partner."

Dana sighed with relief, thanking their good luck that she and Sarah hadn't played a round of golf. They needed to bury their clubs deep in the motorhome's storage compartment before anyone asked about them.

As they watched the others line up, Sarah asked, "Should we go inside?"

"We haven't played golf so let's keep a low profile."

"We discovered the body, Dana. We're already in the limelight."

"True, but not suspects… I guess you're right. We'd better go inside." Joining the other golfers in line, they waited several moments before they were escorted to a long table covered with pens and forms. Golfers were already filling them out, wherever they could find a place to perch. Dana made eye contact with the young deputy who had chauffeured them to the resort from the sheriff's office. Leaving the registration table, the short, sandy haired young deputy walked over.

"You two golfers?"

They slowly shook their heads.

"Sheriff said if you were, he wants to talk to you again."

Dana asked why. "We haven't played golf since we've been here."

"Doesn't matter. Anyone could have hit that ball from anywhere in the resort."

"But the Zagori woman was nearly undressed when we found her."

"Maybe somebody wanted to make it look like a sex crime," he said.

Sarah was fuming. "Why would two sixty-year-old widows kill a woman they didn't even know? We're just learning to play golf and we can't drive a ball accurately enough to kill someone at a distance."

"Nobody said it was from a distance."

It was Dana's turn to gasp. "You mean that someone deliberately drove a ball into her head?"

"That's not for me to say, but I've been instructed to have a look at your golf equipment."

"Be our guests," Sarah did an about face to lead the way to the entrance.

Once outside, they were told to seat themselves in the back of his patrol car, which appeared blocked in by golf carts. Dana could hear their escort swearing as he tried to move the cart parked ahead of him.

"No one's going to have anything to do with us now," Sarah complained.

Dana locked her seatbelt. "I wouldn't worry about that now. It appears that we're the county's number one suspects."

"How could this have happened?"

Dana watched the deputy return to the clubhouse, probably to ticket the golf cart owner who had blocked him in. Relaxing against the seat, she told Sarah they had nothing to worry about. There was no evidence to connect them with the murder.

Moments later, the deputy appeared with an older couple in tow. They seemed to be apologizing, although the deputy must have pulled in behind their cart. When the golf cart had been laboriously moved, inch by inch to avoid the others surrounding it, the deputy climbed behind the wheel and they slowly left the clubhouse.

This is insane, Dana thought when they reached the motorhome. *But it'll soon be over.* Exiting the patrol car, she retrieved the RV keys from her pocket and unlocked the storage compartment. She noticed scratches around the lock and pointed them out to the deputy.

The deputy lifted the compartment door, telling them not to move. Dana was glad they hadn't hidden the golf clubs, which would have made him suspicious. Placing Sarah's bag on the concrete pad, he told them to be seated in the patio chairs while he inspected each club. In the process a small black object fell to the ground.

Picking it up, he said, "What's this? A spare pair of lace panties?" Stretching the spandex, he looked from them to both women. "I doubt either one of you could fit in these."

Dana felt light-headed, glad that she was sitting down. The lingerie didn't belong to either one of them, and a sinking feeling in her stomach told her who the owner was.

Retrieving an evidence bag, he dropped the lingerie

inside before returning for Dana's golf bag. She could hear the dog barking inside the coach but there was nothing she could do to calm her.

Instead of pulling each club from the bag, he turned it upside down, the club heads striking the concrete. A skimpy black lace bra lay among the clubs.

Chapter Five

"Looks like a matching set." A black lace bra dangled from a seven iron. "I suppose it belongs to you, Miz Logan?" It was obviously too small for Sarah.

She hesitated. "Probably not my size."

"I wonder who it belongs to." The bra deposited in the evidence bag, he opened the car to reach for his microphone. They could hear him calling for backup. "Two female perps ready for transport."

When he returned, Sarah pleaded, "Let us feed our dog and allow her do her business before we leave."

"I've got your keys. I'll call the pound. They'll take care of her."

Sarah wailed, "You can't do that to Jenny."

Dana explained that Jenny was a domesticated wolf. She might not go willingly with a stranger.

"Wolves aren't allowed in RV parks. We'll have to tranquilizer her and take her in."

After all the travails they'd been through, Dana feared this case would be their worst. Frustrated, she resisted the urge to kick him when he pulled her from the chair.

The deputy removed a pair of handcuffs from his belt and clicked a bracelet on one of their wrists, tethering them together.

"You're making a mistake," Sarah said as he unlocked the trunk of his patrol car.

"Please don't do this," Dana said. "My friend's right. You're making a terrible mistake."

Ignoring their pleas, he led them to the back seat of the patrol car, telling Dana to be seated first. When everyone was buckled in, he backed from the lot before calling animal control.

"Why in heaven's name would you suspect two older women on vacation, who didn't even know the victim?" Sarah said when they left the resort.

He muttered to himself. "Two women traveling together looking for victims." Angrier than Dana had ever seen her, Sarah said, "You're wasting your time and ours by not going after the real killer."

"Stay calm," Dana said. "We'll straighten this all out when we reach the sheriff's office. Even if I have to call Walter."

"I thought you didn't want him to know where you are."

"He might have to come to our rescue, Sarah, if we can't convince the sheriff that we're innocent."

Sarah's red face faded to pink as she sighed and leaned her head against the seat. "I don't know why you've run away from him for so long, Dana. The man's a hunk who's clearly in love with you. And you know he'll drop everything to come."

"He's due to retire next month. I'm sure he has a lot to wrap up before he leaves office."

"So you'd rather wither in jail until after he's no longer sheriff and can't help us?"

"Of course not. It's just that—"

"What? That you're embarrassed that he has to come to our rescue again?"

"He hasn't always come to our rescue, Sarah. He helped us while we were investigating, but we're the ones who solved the murders."

"Don't forget your daughter, Kerrie."

"We're not calling her in on this case. She has a life now with Tom and a baby on the way."

"I know you're disappointed they eloped, but it's exciting that you're about to become a grandmother."

Dana's smile was brief. She worried that Kerrie would lose the baby if she came to lend her expertise. Closing her eyes, she tried to think herself out of their dilemma, but the trip ended before an answer presented itself. The door opened and they were pulled from the patrol car and led into an anteroom still handcuffed together. Sarah complained to anyone who would listen.

After they were processed and locked in a holding cell, they waited nearly an hour before an investigator had time to see them. When they entered the small interrogation room, Dana asked that they be relieved of their constraints.

"We're innocent," Sarah insisted before he could say a word.

"That's not what the evidence says."

Dana sighed and briefly closed her eyes. "We've helped to solve nearly ten murders, and we're not stupid enough to leave blatant evidence in our golf bags."

"Really?" He was obviously unconvinced.

"I hate to drag our friend, Sheriff Grayson, into this case, but he can certainly vouch for us." She gave him Walter's cell number and waited for his reaction. She knew Walter would be annoyed that she hadn't told him about their vacation trip.

When he punched in the number, Dana listened as the investigator briefly explained the reason for his call. Dana could hear Walter's shocked voice when the officer held the phone away from his ear. After several minutes of uh-huhs and head nodding, the investigator handed Dana the phone.

Hesitantly accepting it, she said, "Walter?"

"What have you two gotten yourselves into this time, Dana?"

"Just another murder case."

"What are you doing in Texas?"

"Sarah and I decided to take a little trip."

"Still tripping over bodies, I hear."

"Actually, we pulled the body from a lake. It's not something we wanted to do during our vacation."

"Let me check my schedule."

She tried to convince him not to come, but knew it was inevitable. She heard papers rattling before he said, "I can be there on Thursday. Try to stay out of trouble until then."

"But all we need is for you to vouch for us."

"I doubt he's going to take my word over the phone."

Dana's heart sank into her knees, imagining herself and Sarah behind bars until Walter arrived. And what would happen to Jenny? She was mild mannered for a wolf, but what if someone antagonized her? Would they euthanize her at the animal control center? A tear slid down her cheek as she handed back the phone.

"What's wrong, Dana?" Handcuffs rattling, Sarah attempted to hug her.

"Walter's coming but I'm worried about Jenny."

The investigator replaced the receiver in its cradle. "Who's Jenny? Your daughter?"

"Our dog. They took her to the pound because your deputy arrested us."

He sighed, still apparently uncertain what to do with them. Motioning them to wait, he hit an intercom button and asked someone to look up Sheriff Grayson's office number. When Walter came back on the line, the deputy explained that he was checking his identity. When he hung up, the deputy said, "Explain how the lingerie got in your golf bags."

Dana told him about the scratches around the storage compartment lock, and that it had been broken into. Their dog had barked early the previous morning, something Jenny rarely did. Dana said she was sure that someone had placed the undergarments in the golf bags to incriminate them.

"Your deputy was premature in arresting us. And no one knows who the lingerie belongs to. We had no reason to kill Varina Zagori, but from what we've heard, there are plenty of people in the resort who wanted her dead."

When asked, they gave him the names of their known suspects and repeated the rumors they'd heard.

Drumming his fingers on his desk, the red haired investigator apologized for the rookie deputy's arrest, but said they were still persons of interest who were not allowed to leave the county. Relieved, they promised to pass on any pertinent information they might unearth.

"Wait here while I run an NCIC on you. If you don't have records, I'll let you go. But leave the investigation to the department, ladies. We don't want someone pulling *your* bodies out of the lake. Sheriff Grayson will be here in a few days. I suggest you stay close to home until he arrives."

The same deputy drove them home but didn't say a word until they reached Paradise Acres. Mumbling an apology, he left. When Dana unlocked the motorhome, they were overjoyed to find Jenny waiting for them.

Maybe animal control hadn't had time to come for her.

Sarah grabbed the leash and hooked it to the dog's collar. "Let's take Jenny for a ride and stay away until after dark, just in case. The wheels of justice move slowly and the dog catcher might not have received the rescind order yet."

Dana agreed and they hurriedly piled into the Jeep. "Where to, partner?"

"Anywhere that's not over the county line."

The dog chuffed softly from the back seat and leaned to lick Sarah's arm. It was if she knew they were in danger.

"Jenny likes tacos, Dana. Why don't we find a Taco Bell in town?"

"Sounds good to me, although my stomach hasn't settled down since the sheriff's office."

"You think we're being followed?"

Dana glanced in the rearview mirror. "I wouldn't be surprised. The investigator may have let us go so they can keep us in their radar."

"They're wasting their time. We have no motive, opportunity or—"

"Lots of innocent people have been convicted of murder and lesser crimes. And have spent decades in prison. Some even die there."

Sarah's voice quavered "We don't have that many years left."

"That's why we need to find out who planted the lingerie in our golf bags."

Sarah said she didn't think the killer was a woman. "Why?"

"How many women are locksmiths?"

"That does narrow it down, although a locksmith wouldn't have scratched the RV's paint."

"Unless he was working in the dark without a

flashlight."

"You're right. It wasn't quite daylight when Jenny barked yesterday morning."

"I guess we'll have to eavesdrop on conversations in the resort. Somebody might have seen the killer sneak onto our lot. Maybe one of the security officers."

Dana remembered a potluck dinner announcement posted on the resort's activities board, planned for the following evening. A good place to listen to local gossip. Sarah was an excellent cook and could whip up something to take along. Glancing again in the side mirror, she noticed a tan car matching the Jeep's lane changes. An unmarked police car? Let them follow. Then again, it could be the killer. They couldn't take anything for granted. She pulled into the fast food drive through lane and watched her rearview mirror, releasing the breath she'd been holding when the car drove past. But would the driver lay in wait?

Jenny waited patiently until they finished their meals. Sarah then held the remains in the wrappers so that the dog could finish them off. When Dana's wrappers had been licked clean, she cautiously pulled into the street and made a quick right turn. No one seemed to have followed.

"I'm glad we're not in Dallas, Sarah. I'm afraid I'd never find our way out of the city."

"We're not allowed to go there, anyway. It's in another county."

"Let's go home and read our Kindles with the lights out so the dog catcher will think we're not there."

"I've got a better idea. We'll go to the grocery store and buy the ingredients for one of your prize winning chocolate cakes for the pot luck dinner tomorrow night."

Sarah smiled. "Sounds good to me."

Jenny woofed and had one ear cocked when Dana looked for her in the rearview mirror.

"Dogs can't eat chocolate," Sarah said. "It makes them sick. But I'll make you a green beans and salmon cake."

The sound Jenny made sounded almost human.

"Too bad we can't take her with us wherever we go. Most people are afraid of wolves. Hopefully that includes the killer."

Dana glanced again in the side mirror. "I'm surprised that no one has complained about her to management."

"Jenny is never off her leash unless she's in the motorhome."

"I know, but she needs exercise."

Sarah patted her stomach. "And so do we. I've gained five pounds since we've been here from nervous overeating."

"I have too. We need to stay in shape."

"You're right about that. Overweight detectives can wind up dead."

"Remember Nero Wolf?"

Sarah nodded. "Rex Stout's detective rarely left his arm chair."

"Unfortunately, we can't solve the murder by sitting in the motorhome. We've got to beat the bushes to find the killer."

Chapter Six

Their walk around the resort was depressing. It seemed they were persona non grata because everyone was ignoring them. Sarah was especially troubled that no one would talk to her. Wiping her forehead with a wrist band, she said, "They can't believe we're guilty just because we left the resort twice in a patrol car."

"There must be some sort of stigma attached to wearing handcuffs."

"Definitely not a current fashion statement."

Back at the motorhome, Dana fanned herself with a newspaper. "Attending the pot luck dinner may be a waste of time, but we can listen in on conversations. The murder must still be what everyone's talking about."

Sarah gathered the ingredients for her chocolate cake. Dana marveled at her cooking skills, especially when she made something special from scratch. Her own baking had been confined to premixed packages.

Tail wagging, Jenny sat watching Sarah sift the ingredients into a large mixing bowl, obviously hoping she would drop something. When the batter slid safely in the oven, Dana reminded her of the fish cake she had promised Jenny.

"Dogs are like elephants. They never forget."

"I know Jenny doesn't forget. Feed her green beans and she's your friend forever." Taking crumbled pieces of salmon from the fridge, Sarah pulled a container of beans from the top shelf and placed the food on the counter. Jenny jumped against her, nearly causing her to lose her balance.

"Down girl, I've got work to do."

"Speaking of work, Sarah, I wonder if Varina had a job and was a full time resort resident."

"I overheard somebody say that she worked part time in the resort store, so she must have been a full timer."

"If *she* had a job, her husband probably works as well. We need to find out where."

"That won't be easy, Dana, if no one will talk to us."

There's a directory that lists all the lot owners."

Sarah stopped what she was doing to stare at her. "You're not thinking of buying a lot, are you?"

"I can always sell it later."

"But, Dana, these lots are expensive. I saw some listed for over two hundred thousand dollars."

"I'll buy a cheap one without all the build-outs and greenery."

"No barbeque or outdoor furniture?"

"We can buy some."

"What if they won't sell you a lot because we're murder suspects?"

Dana sighed. "In this depressed market, I'm sure they'd sell to Jack the Ripper, if he had the cash."

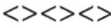

48

An hour and a half later, Sarah carefully balanced the chocolate cake on her lap while Dana drove them to the clubhouse. They arrived fifteen minutes early to find a table in the middle of the room where they could eavesdrop on conversations. A large woman with ink black hair frowned when Sarah placed her cake on the dessert table. Expecting the chilly reception, they took their seats at the table, facing the entrance.

"Nobody's going to sit with us, Dana."

"Keep smiling and you may be surprised. People will eventually give into their curiosity."

The tables around them were nearly filled when a slender, white haired man asked if he could join them. Dana guessed his age at eighty. Patting the chair next to her, Sarah told him they would be happy to have him as a dinner companion. His grateful smile made him a welcome companion. Was he curious or did he not know about them?

He extended his hand. "Pat Petersen. And who might you lovely ladies be?"

"Dana Logan and Sarah Cafferty."

Grinning broadly, he said, "You look like those actors, Gina Davis and Kathy Bates."

Sarah giggled. "Thank you, Pat. I'm flattered. People always say that Dana looks like Gina, but I've never been compared to Kathy Bates."

Dana smiled. "You do, actually. I guess I never noticed." Turning to their dinner companion, she asked if he were a longtime resident of the resort. He acknowledged that he was, but said he had been visiting his daughter in Kansas until that morning.

"So you haven't heard about the murder?"

"Oh, sure. Bad news travels fast in this place."

"Who do you think may have killed Varina," Sarah asked.

"Coulda been anybody. She was a wild one."

Dana's sigh was heavy. They couldn't eavesdrop on others with Pat at their table. They might as well ask him as many questions as he was willing to answer. Did he know Varina's husband?

He nodded. "Nice guy but a little naïve, if you know what I mean."

"How so, Pat?"

He paused, probably deciding how much he should say. "She was kind of a loose cannon and he was her anchor. Why he let her get away with fooling around is beyond me. I woulda smacked her upside her head and told her to behave."

"Did anyone in particular have it in for her?" Sarah asked.

He grinned. "It would be easier to tell you who didn't."

"Was it just her infidelities that turned people off?"

"Oh, no, it was her attitude. She was always talking trash about other people. Then, if somebody got their back up about it, she would turn on the charm and smile till her face cracked."

Sarah gently patted his hand. "A real hypocrite, eh?"

"You could say that."

A stout, gray haired woman appeared at their table and leaned to talk to Pat. "You're in the wrong place, dear." She gripped his arm, pulling him to his feet. "Everyone's waiting for you over there." She indicated a table along the far wall.

Blushing, he said, "Sorry, ladies. It was nice talking to you."

The stout woman glared at Sarah before leading Pat away.

Sarah grimaced. "Poor man's in trouble for sitting here."

"He told us all he could," Dana whispered. "Now we can eavesdrop at our leisure."

"Everyone's getting in line for the pot luck buffet. I guess we'd better join them."

They took their place in line behind a tall, fortyish man and petite, raven haired woman who didn't quite reach his shoulder. Engaged in conversation, they were probably unaware of the new arrivals. Their discussion evolved from their afternoon golf game to the latest resort scandal.

"Who do you think did it?" the woman asked.

"Who knows? It could have been Paul or Camille or Dennis or anyone else in the club."

"Who was she doing before she died?"

"I heard it was Stan."

"He's old enough to have been her father."

"He drives a million dollar Prevost."

"Ah, a sugar daddy."

Dana shivered. These people were talking about the murder victim as though reciting a grocery list. They didn't seem the least bit shocked by Varina's indiscretions.

Sarah nudged her and indicated another couple at a nearby table, who were already eating dinner. "Do they look familiar?"

"Not really."

"She's a member of the photography club and he's the realtor who showed us around. I wonder why he never came back."

Dana squinted for a better look. "You're right. I didn't recognize him in a golf shirt instead of his business suit. He's wearing glasses and his hair's combed over."

Sarah waved and was promptly ignored. "I'm surprised we haven't been asked to leave the clubhouse."

"The night's not over yet."

An attractive, distinguished appearing, middle aged man touched Dana's shoulder. Smiling, he asked that they join him at the director's table. Introducing himself as Gerald McKinsey, he said, "I noticed that you ladies are dining alone."

Sarah looked as though she were going to faint. "Director's table?"

"The one nearest the stage," he said nodding in that direction. Dana noticed two empty chairs at an otherwise crowded table.

"We'd love to join you," Sarah said, glancing at Dana for approval.

Dana thanked him and they watched as he threaded his way among the tables to his own. Then, sitting next to a pretty, blond woman; he leaned to whisper in her ear. Was that his wife? What in the world was going on?

When the line reached the buffet table, Sarah quickly filled her plate to capacity but Dana's stomach still churned with anxiety. Depending on what transpired at the director's table, their ostracism could evaporate. Dana partially filled her plate with jello and a tossed salad. She then followed Sarah to the table.

Gerald McKinsey and two other men got to their feet when they arrived. Smiling, they introduced their companions, all members of the board of directors. Dana thought this was akin to dining at the captain's table during a holiday cruise.

Marie McKinsey, the director's wife, asked where they were from and why they had chosen Paradise Acres. When told, she seemed to think Wyoming was an exotic place.

Sarah laughed. "It's beautiful during the warmer months but in winter you can freeze your—"

"We're native Californians," Dana cut in. "And Sarah hasn't quite become acclimatized."

A slender brunette, whose name Dana couldn't recall, said, "Aren't you the ones who found the body?"

So that's the reason for the invitation. Dana briefly told them about Sarah's discovery, making eye contact with everyone present.

"It was quite a shock to find a body instead of a diving duck," her friend said. "I can't imagine that happening in a gorgeous place like this."

The director and his wife lowered their eyes. "It's never happened before," McKinsey said, "and I'm sure it won't again. By the way, are you interested in becoming property owners?"

Dana nodded. "We were shown around the resort by a realtor who never returned." She cringed when Sarah told them about the other residents not speaking to them.

McKinsey cleared his throat. "We heard about that and thought that if you dined with us—"

Dana thanked him and said she was definitely interested in buying property there, although she still hadn't decided if she would actually go through with the purchase. It depended on whether they were accepted into the community.

McKinsey smiled and excused himself. Taking the stage, he announced a director's meeting following the dinner, and briefly filled the lot owners in on impending business. Dana compared him favorably with the mayor of a small village. But was he really as kind and considerate as he seemed? She glanced at his wife, noticing her wink and smile at the man across the table from her. Was this Peyton Place or actually a caring community?

Sarah appeared to be nodding off after her heavy meal, so Dana suggested they leave for home. The others seemed genuinely disappointed, and she wondered if there was someone among them they could befriend. Before they left, she invited their hosts over for a glass of wine the following evening, and was surprised when they accepted.

Riding back to the motorhome in the golf cart, Sarah wondered if someone was setting them up. "No one's going to tell us who the murderer is, Dana, although everyone seems to know everything that goes on in this place. I'm worried that we're going to be patsies."

"I haven't heard that term in years. You're showing your age, my friend."

"Oh, who cares. I just wanna go home and not worry about diving ducks and dead bodies."

"So you don't think I should buy a lot here?"

"Are you serious? I don't think we'd ever fit in."

Dana drove the golf cart onto their lot and pulled the key from the ignition. "A good night's sleep is what we need. Tomorrow we'll brainstorm about our next move."

A note was taped to their door, barely visible in the lamplight at the front of the lot. Dana pealed it off and unlocked the motorhome. Jenny was barking and needed some TLC, which Sarah sleepily provided by stooping to pet the dog. Dana flicked on an overhead light to read the note. Printed in block letters, it said, *If you want to know who left the underwear in your golf bags meet me at the big swimming pool at midnight.*

"You're not considering going, are you Dana?"

"Of course not. Unless we take someone from security along."

"If this were legit, the person would have called or stopped by during the day."

"I don't trust anyone in this place, not even security."

Sarah reminded her that Walter would arrive in two days.

Dana's cell phone rang and she looked at the caller ID. "Speaking of Walter—"

His voice was soft and reassuring when he asked how they were doing. Dana almost wished he were there to take her in his arms. Almost because she didn't want him scolding her for not informing him of their trip.

"Any leads?" he asked after he said he missed her.

"Not many. There are too many suspects and tight-lipped people here. My impression is that although they disliked the victim, they're protecting both her and the killer."

"That's odd. No one's talking about the case?"

"Not really. All we actually know is that she wasn't a nice persons and someone killed her with a golf ball."

Walter laughed. "You can fill me in on the particulars when I get there. I can't wait to see you."

Dana smiled at her cell. "And I you. We'll pick you up at the airport on Thursday."

He gave her his flight number and time of arrival, said he loved her, and clicked off.

"Why didn't you tell him about the note, Dana?"

"Because he would have dropped everything and taken the next flight. I don't want to jeopardize his last days in office or his retirement."

"That still leaves the note. Who could have written it? Someone who's playing a practical joke?"

Dana retrieved her cell phone. "I'll call security and ask that they check it out."

"Good thinking, Detective Logan. I hope whoever takes the call isn't the killer."

"I'm afraid we'll have to take that chance."

Chapter Seven

The phone rang six times before a gruff voice barked *hello*. Dana hesitated, stunned by his abrasive attitude.

"Security?" she asked.

"Yeah."

Telling him about the note, she asked that he find out who was waiting at the pool, or notify the sheriff's office. When he said he'd stop by for the note, she said that wasn't a good idea. The killer was probably watching their motorhome and wouldn't show up for the meeting. She could hear him grumbling to himself. She could also hear a TV blaring in the background.

"Okay, I'll call the sheriff's office."

"On second thought, I'd better call so I can read an officer the note."

"Suit yourself." She heard the receiver fall into its cradle.

Dana punched in 911. When a dispatcher answered, she told her about the note and asked to speak to an investigator. She was told to call the non-emergency number.

"But this *is* an emergency. The killer's waiting for me at the swimming pool."

"I suggest that you don't go."

Dana clicked off and punched in the number she'd been given. When a deputy answered, she explained the situation and asked that he arrive without a siren or flashing lights.

"Are you sure it's not a joke, ma'am?"

"Positive. Someone planted incriminating evidence in our golf bags."

"It's a quarter after eleven. I'm not sure I can make it in time."

"Then *we'll* go. I have a permit to carry and my friend has a regulation baseball bat."

"Not a good idea. I'll be there as soon as I can."

She heard the disconnect and sank into her recliner chair. "Have you noticed how uncaring people are becoming, Sarah?"

"Oh, you mean newspapers tossed on the roof and old ladies knocked down on street corners?"

"I was referring to security."

"I'm sure they get a lot of nonsense calls. And he was probably watching a sporting event."

"Murder cases should receive priority."

"You're not thinking of going over there, are you, Dana?"

"What if the deputy doesn't arrive in time? The killer will get away."

Sarah plopped down in the chair beside her. "Think about this: Varina Zagori was found in the lake and the killer wants us to meet him at the pool. Does that sound like he plans to drown us? He seems to have a fixation with water."

"Or she?"

"I have a hard time believing it's a woman."

Dana lowered her recliner's foot rest. "It's entirely possible that a jealous wife committed the murder. I imagine there's more than one of them living in the resort."

"We need to get our hands on a property owners' directory. I think one of Varina's neighbors may have killed her."

Dana vacated her chair. "We still need to get a glimpse of whoever wrote that note."

Sighing, Sarah followed her to the closet where they retrieved dark, lightweight sweatshirts and baseball caps. Their sandals were then exchanged for black tennis shoes, which had become standard equipment for their various trips. Sarah picked up her bat and Dana chambered shells into her revolver. But would they be able to sneak from the motorhome, without being seen? She slipped the short-barreled revolver into her small, flesh-colored holster, which she clipped inside her waistband.

The autumn night was cool, the moon only a sliver when Dana crept through the partially opened door to squint into the darkness. She knew someone could be hiding between RVs, and re-scanned the area looking for movement. Beckoning to Sarah, she quietly climbed down the steps and into the blackness behind the coach and waited as Sarah locked the door. They had plenty of time to walk to the far side of the resort, so they waited several moments before slipping along the back of the neighboring lots. Dana tripped over a hose and nearly lost her balance.

"Let's go back," Sarah whispered. "This is insane."

"We'll never feel safe until the killer's in prison. Go back if you want. I've got to see who wrote the note."

Sarah hesitated before she followed. When they reached the first intersection, Dana noticed that all but one of the RVs were unlighted. The pot luck dinner must have broken up early and those who attended were probably now asleep. She could hear Sarah's frightened breathing behind her and turned back to place a hand on her shoulder.

"Not much further," she whispered.

Sarah knelt on someone's grass. Tenting her fingers, she said a silent prayer. Not a bad idea. Dana followed suit, asking that she be allowed to see the killer but not make contact with her. She hoped that prayers were answered 24/7.

The swimming pool was directly ahead, enclosed in a wrought iron fence. They crouched, straining their eyes, wishing for night vision goggles. Sarah pointed to a large tree across the street and they crept hunched over toward it. When they reached the other side, Dana noticed a car driving toward them with its lights off. Was it the deputy or the killer? They crouched behind the thick-trunked tree and watched as the car drove past toward the pool. If it were the deputy, he should have parked blocks away.

They watched and waited for nearly an hour before starting back to the motorhome. Maybe the note had been someone's joke. Fast walking in the street, they arrived home to find a patrol car parked out front, a deputy waiting for them. He said he hadn't seen anyone near the pool and wanted to read the note. They agreed and led the way to the motorhome door, which they found unlocked. Once inside they discovered Jenny missing as well as the note.

"We were tricked," Sarah wailed.

The young, broad-shoulder deputy looked about the RV and remarked that it appeared to have been vandalized. "I advised you not to go to the pool."

Dana twisted Jenny's leash. "We've got to find our

dog."

"She'll come back when she's hungry," he said. "Tell me about the note."

Dana knew what had been written by heart and recited it for him.

"Stay put and lock your door. I'll take a look for the dog."

Sarah told him that locking the door wouldn't help. The killer was adept at picking locks.

"Then you need to come to the station for protective custody."

Both women insisted they weren't going anywhere until their dog returned. When the deputy left, Sarah asked, "Do you think Jenny's looking for her puppies?"

"Maybe. You know we couldn't keep them."

Sarah sighed. "I'm glad they're with good people. Gus and Marietta love them dearly. I know they're one big happy family."

It was five minutes after four that morning when a knock at the door awakened Dana, who had fallen asleep in her chair. Sarah softly snored in her own recliner beside her. Tiptoeing to the door, she gripped Sarah's heavy bat and asked who was there.

"Deputy O'Donnel. I found your dog."

Setting the bat aside, she hurriedly unlocked the door. The deputy let go of Jenny's collar and she bounded up the steps.

"Where did you find her?"

"Sniffing around your motorhome."

"But she didn't bark."

"You know her better than I do... Mind if I come in? There's something I need to talk to you about."

Dana stepped aside as he climbed the steps. She heard Sarah shriek when Jenny jumped into her lap, waking her.

The deputy stood ramrod tall in their small living space until Dana asked that he take a seat on the couch. Folding his hands he said, "You ladies aren't safe with a killer running loose. I need to take you in."

Sarah clapped palms on her knees. "Three trips to town in a patrol car will ruin our reputations here forever."

"Better that than dead, ma'am."

"I don't think we're the intended victims," Dana said. "The killer's trying to pin the murder on *us*. If we're found dead, your department will be looking closer at everyone in the resort."

O'Donnel appeared thoughtful. "You could be right, but—"

"I'm well trained with firearms and Sarah could serve as a substitute batter for the Dodgers. We can take care of ourselves."

Jenny woofed her agreement, her tail striking the floor like a metronome.

The deputy reluctantly left, insisting they call the sheriff's department if there were additional notes or break-ins. When Dana locked the door behind him, they trooped off to bed. They would plan their next move later that day.

When Jenny woke them at 6:30 that morning, Dana volunteered to take her out. It seemed she had only closed her eyes when she heard the dog's sharp bark. They would have to stay with Jenny every moment she was outside, so Dana donned her robe and tied the dog's leash to a hook on the motorhome's outer wall. She then took a seat in a patio chair. Yawning, she spotted something waving in the early morning breeze. It seemed caught in the storage compartment door.

Grabbing the material she pulled. The fabric refused to budge but a large silver button fell into her hand. The button was unfamiliar and had an unusual design. Jenny was still sniffing the ground when Dana went back inside. Sarah was asleep, so she dropped the button in her pocket and called the sheriff's department before returning to the patio. Once there she discovered Jenny missing. Was someone playing games? Or had the dog learned to escape? Climbing back inside, she woke Sarah.

Yawning, her friend followed her to the patio where she noticed the dog's collar still attached to the leash. "She slipped her collar like Houdini, Dana. I hope someone didn't take her."

Dana walked to the other side of the coach, softy calling Jenny's name. She found her chewing on something behind the coach that she must have found in the grass. When she was able to wrestle the object away from the dog, she realized it was a well chewed dagger sheath. Jenny wasn't happy that she'd been relieved of her new toy. Her sharp bark had undoubtedly awakened the neighbors.

Holding the sheath a few inches from her nose, Dana led the dog back to her leash. Sarah had already tightened the collar and was ready to buckle it around Jenny's neck. When the collar was secure, she asked what Dana was carrying.

Dana shivered when she handed her the sheath. "I'm glad we weren't here when the killer removed the dagger. She must have dropped it in the dark and couldn't find it."

"But don't these things clip on the belt like your holster?"

"If it were a woman with elastic waisted pants, she wouldn't have had anywhere to hang the knife. And look at the sheath. It's the same shade of green as the grass, so it would have been hard to find at night, even with a flashlight."

Sarah smoothed the sheath on the patio table. "Why do you insist it's a woman?"

"Look how small the sheath is. A man would carry a bigger knife."

"Unless it's a small man... Let's go inside before the neighbors string us up for disturbing their sleep."

Dana brewed them each a cup of chai tea and they settled in their recliners. It was still early but they were both too keyed to go to bed.

"Most people who carry knives don't arm themselves with guns," Dana said. "What worries me is that whoever was carrying the knife had it out of the sheath and ready to use."

Sarah gasped. "He could have used it on Jenny."

"The dog must have bolted from the motorhome the second the door was opened, thinking it was us."

Sarah held up the battered sheath. "This isn't much evidence to go on."

"But this is." Dana pulled the large button from her pocket. "I nearly forgot. There's something hanging from the storage compartment door that was attached to this."

Sarah took the button and turned it over in her hand. "A phoenix rising from the ashes? I haven't seen one of these in years."

"Where did you see one?"

"On an old uniform in a California museum."

Dana grabbed the RV keys and opened the storage

compartment door. "We need to see what the killer planted this time."

The neighbors in the next lot were leaving. Hopefully they wouldn't report them for making too much noise. Dana touched the gray material that had been hanging from the door. Closing the compartment, she took a closer look.

"This appears to be a woman's vest, Sarah."

"I think you're right. A slender woman. Maybe a size four."

"Or even a child's vest. I wonder if Varina had a daughter. Or a grandchild."

"If she married young, she might have been old enough to have a grandchild."

They climbed back into the motorhome where Sarah prepared them French toast. While they were finishing breakfast, someone knocked at the door. It wasn't the same deputy but he had obviously been thoroughly briefed.

"Why do you think someone's leaving clues?" he asked. "And why here in your motorhome?" His deep brown eyes seemed to bore into Dana.

"Probably because we found the body. Who better to pin the murder on?"

He lifted his cap to brush gray hair from his forehead. "I've read the reports of this case and there seems to be plenty of suspects—people who were well acquainted with the victim."

"Exactly," Sarah said. "We've been trying to find out who had the motive and opportunity. We already know the means."

The deputy warned them about investigating on their own. The knife sheath was a warning, he said. If they had been at home, they might have been the next victims.

He left with the sheath, vest and button after taking a brief report. He too suggested protective custody, but Dana told him that her friend, Sheriff Grayson, was flying in the following morning. They would stay safe until then.

When he left, they both collapsed in their chairs. Maybe they *should* leave the investigation to the police. But how could they sit in the motorhome knowing a killer was roaming the resort, planning to plant more evidence against them?

Sarah had already dozed off, so brainstorming was out of the question. The McKinseys were coming for a visit that evening and they needed to prepare something special. Would they provide answers to the mystery, and why had they accepted her invitation? Nothing made sense, especially her nagging suspicion that the killer was a woman.

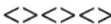

Dana was taking inventory of the refrigerator when Sarah awoke from her nap. "Hungry already? I thought my French toast would last until noon."

"The McKinsey's are coming. Do we need to go shopping?"

"I thought you promised the deputy we wouldn't leave our lot."

Dana asked her to whip up something fit for the director and his wife from supplies on hand. "McKinsey seems to have his fingers on all the buttons in this resort. If he doesn't know who wanted to kill Varina Zagori, no one does."

"I think you're right, and I'm curious why they're befriending us. Could they be part of a conspiracy?"

"Maybe they want to find out what we know, Sarah."

"We know nothing. We're just curious about the body we pulled from the lake."

Dana walked to the window to peer outside. "Exactly. Two aging widows only interested in enjoying their vacation."

"You think they'll believe it?"

"Not if they've talked to members of the photography club."

"Telling them was a mistake, Dana."

"I know, but we can honestly say that we're afraid the killer's after us. And that we've given up our plan to identify whoever it is." She patted Sarah's shoulder. "I'll finish cleaning up while you whip up something special for our guests."

"Too bad we don't have truth serum to spike their wine. There's entirely too much skullduggery going on in this place."

<><><>

Late that afternoon as the sun was sinking toward the horizon, Sarah carried a plate of hors d'oeuvres to the patio table, which Dana had covered with a festive red tablecloth and freshly polished wine glasses. Checking her watch, she glanced up to see a golf cart pull onto their lot. Their guests had arrived.

Tall, distinguished Gerald McKinsey helped his pretty, blond wife from the cart. Taking her hand, he led her to their hosts. What a handsome couple they were. Smiling, they offered both women a brief hug.

Once they were seated, Dana handed McKinsey a bottle of wine to inspect.

Smiling, he said, "You have exquisite tastes. Where did you find this bottle of Chateau Margaux?"

"I found it in Cheyenne. I've been saving it for a

special occasion."

"I'm flattered that you would share it with us, Dana."
He handed the bottle to his wife, Marie.

"Ah, nineteen ninety-five. Blackberry and cassis,
an elegant choice," she said. "Did you know that this
vineyard was founded a thousand years ago?"

Dana sighed. *Thank heavens they appreciate this
smooth, expensive wine. I'm glad I brought it along.*
She nodded. "They've definitely mastered the art of
wine making."

Would the dark ambrosia prompt them to open up
about the murder? Gerald sniffed his wine and swished
it around in his mouth before swallowing. His smile
was one of pure pleasure. "Tell me, ladies, why did you
choose Paradise Acres?"

"Sarah found it on the Internet and we thought it
was a perfect vacation spot."

"But little did we know what we were getting into."
Sarah muttered beneath her breath. Dana heard her
and nearly choked on her wine.

If the McKinseys heard, they pretended nothing
had been said.

"I'm sorry you encountered such a dreadful start to
your vacation," Marie said, studying her wine. "Nothing
like this has happened here before."

"Do you have any inkling who might have killed
Varina Zagori?" Dana asked quietly.

"We don't have a clue," he said. "We understand
that you've been investigating on your own. Have you
learned anything that might help the authorities?"

Sarah delicately reached for an hors d'oeuvre. "Not
really. We were hoping that you might have heard
something."

The director looked to his wife and slightly shook
his head. "We would have reported it to the sheriff if

we knew anything."

Dana asked if the Zagoris were long-time residents of the resort, and was told they had been in residence at least three years. Jerome Zagori was employed as an electronics store manager and his wife had worked part time.

"She was quite outgoing and seemed to like the company of a number of people," Marie said. "I guess that's why she worked a few days a week in the small grocery here in the resort."

"So she had no enemies?"

"Well—" the director said. "I wouldn't say that. We don't engage in gossip but we can't help but hear it."

Dana leaned in closer. "Did someone dislike her?"

"Oh, plenty of people," Marie said. "Varina had an abrasive personality and didn't mind hurting others' feelings."

"I wonder why the store owner would hire someone like her."

"We wondered too, but Harold seemed to like her."

"Harold?"

"The store owner."

"Even though she turned off customers?"

The McKinseys glanced at one another and shrugged. Gerald then looked at his watch. "This has been lovely, but we have a dinner engagement in twenty minutes."

Marie appeared relieved. "Yes, sorry we have to leave so early. You must come and visit us some time."

When they were gone, Sarah insisted that the McKinseys knew who the killer was. "What a shame to waste your bottle of Chateau Margaux."

"It wasn't a waste, Sarah. We now know that they're protecting someone although they didn't approve of the Zagori woman."

"Well, duh. Who did?"

Dana frowned. "I forgot to ask the office manager's name."

"As much as I hate to say this, Dana, it appears you'll have to buy one of the lots to get our hands on the directory."

"You're probably right. Now all we have to do is find that strange realtor, Paul Gates, and insist that he sell us a lot."

"I've never known a real estate agent who didn't follow up on a lead. What do you suppose he's afraid of?"

Chapter Eight

"We'd better get ready, Dana. What are you wearing?"

Clothes were the least of her worries. She didn't have to impress Walter. What she was most concerned with were the recurring visits from the suspected killer. She also wondered about the significance of the phoenix button. Was it a replica of the ones Sarah had seen in the museum, and had the vest belonged to the murder victim? She hoped the sheriff's department could determine its origin.

<><><>

They arrived at Dallas-Fort Worth International Airport an hour before Walter's plane was due to arrive, thankful they had been granted permission to cross the county line. Sarah wanted to browse the shops in Terminal A so they rode the Skylink. Along the way they spotted a sign which said the airport was animal friendly. Sarah bemoaned the fact that they hadn't taken Jenny with them.

"She's better off at home. The killer won't try to break into the motorhome in broad daylight. Not after the mess he made searching for the note."

Sarah's frown deepened. "Or was he searching for something else? Maybe he forgot to wear gloves while he was writing the note. And speaking of the mess, I'm glad we had time to clean it up before Walter gets here. By the way, where's he's going to sleep?"

"If not on the couch, he'll have to rent an RV."

Sarah smiled impishly. "I think he's too big for our couch, and I know you won't let him share your bunk."

Dana noticed Walter walking rapidly toward them, carrying an overnight bag.

"Looks like he's not planning to stay long."

"I'm surprised that he managed any time off at all, Sarah."

"This time he's got good reason to come to our rescue."

Walter dropped his bag and enveloped Dana in his arms. He then gave her a resounding kiss. "Great to see you, Love."

Glad to see him, she enjoyed the warmth of his embrace. She knew she loved him, but marriage? Why did he have to pressure her into a relationship she wasn't ready for?

Dressed in civilian clothes instead of his uniform, he resembled an aging movie star. He even sported a mustache. Walter was grayer at the temples, which made him even more handsome. Was she foolish in not accepting his proposal? What if he met someone in California and forgot about her?

Sarah held her arms wide and accepted a hug. Dana knew that her friend was still attracted to Walter, and often wished that he felt the same about her. Sarah would marry him in a nanosecond.

He was looking at Dana with that lovesick expression she hated. Taking her arm, he said, "Shall we go, ladies?"

They nearly had to jog to keep up with him. Why was he in such a hurry? Dana knew he hated airports, but she had planned an early lunch at one of the nicer restaurants. When she asked if he were hungry, he shook his head no.

Once they reached the Jeep, he hugged her again and offered to drive. Dana insisted that he relax in the passenger seat after his long flight. He'd never traveled to Texas and she wanted him to enjoy the scenery.

"Why Texas, Dana? And why didn't you tell me you were leaving Wyoming?"

"It was just a whim. Sarah and I were getting bored and the lone star state sounded as good as any place to visit."

"It didn't take you long to pull a body from the water."

She glanced at him briefly to determine his mood. "What can I say, Walter? We're magnets for murder. No matter where we go—"

His sigh was heavy. "Is this amateur sleuthing going to continue after we're married?"

Dana shook her head. "I haven't accepted your proposal."

He grinned. "But you know you will."

"That's what I love about you, Walter. You won't take no for an answer."

Sarah coughed from the back seat. "Why don't you drop me off at the motorhome and take a drive by yourselves."

Dana looked at her friend in the rearview mirror. "Because it's not safe to leave you alone."

Walter shifted in the seat to face her. "If it's that dangerous, you both need to stay somewhere else."

When Dana told him they couldn't leave the county, he said he would have a talk with the local sheriff. Dana changed the subject by asking him about the cases he was working on as they drove back to Paradise Acres. He glossed over two murder cases, one of them committed by a suspected psycho who had recently escaped from prison. His original jovial mood had vanished.

When they reached the motorhome, Jenny greeted him by jumping against him and licking his face. At least that brought a smile.

"I'm glad you still have her," he said, stroking Jenny's fur. "She's good protection against an intruder."

Sarah laughed. "The last intruder managed to let her escape."

Dana cringed, wishing Sarah had kept that bit of information to herself. A deep line formed between Walter's eyes and she knew what he was thinking. They needed a man to protect them. Motioning him to be seated, she asked Sarah to make them coffee while she filled Walter in on the latest developments. He said nothing but seemed to be taking mental notes.

When Dana finished, he said, "Does the victim have a police record?"

Dana gasped. "That never occurred to me."

"You must have been too busy interviewing your new neighbors to investigate the victim."

"You're right about that." Sarah handed him a cup of instant coffee. "Dana even wasted a $450 bottle of Chateau Marguax on the resort director and his wife, hoping they could tell us about the killer."

Walter groaned. "I was hoping you were saving the Marguax for our engagement party."

Dana laughed. "That's not the last bottle on earth."

"I'm surprised you haven't spent all your inheritance on your murder solving hobby."

"This is probably the last case Sarah and I will ever investigate."

"I hope you mean that. You're not a cat with nine lives. Whoever's trying to frame you may decide to make your deaths look like a murder-suicide."

Sarah gasped. "We hadn't thought of that, either."

Walter was right. She should have checked out Varina Zagori's background. Dana retrieved her laptop from the small desk and booted up. Accessing her favorite people finder website, she scrolled through the list of Zagoris until she found the victim. She then paid the fee to research her background. There it was in black and white. Varina Zagori, nee Whiting, had been convicted of blackmail and sentenced to five years in prison.

"Looks like she only served three and a half years of her sentence and was released on good behavior," Walter said.

Sarah grimaced. "Varina probably charmed the warden."

Walter's expression was one of concern. "She might have been blackmailing the killer, who decided on a fatal last payment."

Dana chewed her lip. "If it *was* a woman who killed her, she removed Varina's undergarments to make it appear that she had been killed by a man. On second thought, she may have discovered Varina in bed with her husband."

"Then the husband knows, Dana. If a man turns up dead—"

"She decided to eliminate the only witness," Dana finished for her.

Walter said that would be too obvious, unless the wife found a way to frame her husband. He then asked how many people lived in the resort.

Dana estimated the residents at well over a thousand, "but they're not all here at the same time. A lot of them are snowbirds."

"Then finding the killer is like discovering the right grain of sand in the Mojave Desert."

"We know, Walter. But someone will let something slip. Sarah and I decided to talk to Varina's neighbors."

"Do you know where she lived?"

"No, but we'll receive a resident directory when I buy a lot."

Walter's expression was one of shock.

"I'll sell the lot as soon as the killer's arrested."

"The killer knows you're investigating, Love. And I doubt a woman would frame her husband if she's planting bogus evidence in your storage compartment."

"And if the killer's a man?" Sarah prompted.

"If the Zagori woman was as promiscuous as you say, you're looking at a lot of men in the resort who could have killed her."

Dana told him about the minister they'd seen talking to Varina's husband. He might know the man's name that Varina was planning to leave her husband for. On second thought, ordained ministers could refuse to divulge information told them by parishioners. Would Sheriff Brandson tell Walter, if *he* knew?

Walter said, "It depends on how much evidence the sheriff is willing to share. If we print Varina Zagori's arrest record, I may be able to trade information. But he might have already conducted a background check on the victim."

Sarah leaned forward, nearly spilling her coffee. "The sheriff said he has four other murder cases pending, so his staff must be spread awfully thin."

Walter promised to make an appointment with the sheriff as soon as he finished his coffee. "Then," he said, "you and I are going to take Sarah's suggestion to go for a drive."

"But we can't leave her alone."

Walter checked his watch. "It's half past noon. She'll be fine for an hour or so. And I noticed that she still has her bat."

Sarah smiled. "I'll stay inside while you're gone. Jenny will protect me."

Dana reluctantly agreed. She knew what Walter had in mind and dreaded the subject. She asked if he were carrying and was assured that he was. "Then I'll leave my revolver here with Sarah."

Sarah was more afraid of the gun than the killer. "Go," she said, shooing them toward the door. "You can call the sheriff's office on the way."

"Yes, ma'am." He gripped Dana's hand and towed her to the Jeep. There was nothing she could do. They were conspiring against her.

Insisting that he drive, he asked, "Where to, Love?"

She pointed the way, then punched in the sheriff's number and handed him the phone. She had already placed the number on her speed dial. The call only lasted a minute. When he clicked off, he said, "Sheriff Brandson's in Weatherford for a meeting. I have an appointment with him tomorrow at three."

"How long are you planning to stay, Walter?"

"As long as necessary."

Dana groaned inwardly.

"You don't seem to realize how much danger you're in."

"This is ridiculous. No one should believe that Sarah and I are responsible for the Zagori woman's death."

"If I remember correctly, the deputy handcuffed you both and hauled you off—"

Dana said that the young rookie had overreacted.

"Everyone knows that the victim was disliked by nearly everyone in the resort, and we now know she was an ex-convict. None of that has anything to do with us."

"What about Zagori's husband? Is he still in the resort?"

"I'm sure he's the prime suspect, Walter. Once I have the directory, we'll know where he lives. I overheard some widows planning to invite him to dinner."

"Not a bad idea. Why don't you do the same?"

"We'll have to locate him first. I don't think anyone's going to tell us where he lives. Property owners are a tight knit group. It's almost like a caste system here. At the moment, we're members of the lower class renters."

Walter said nothing for several moments, seeming to concentrate on the road. He then said, "I'm sure you know what I need to talk to you about."

"This is not the time to discuss our future together. We're so embroiled in this murder case that I can't think of anything else."

He reminded her of the fact that he was retiring the following month and needed to make plans to leave California. What would she have him do? Stay in a hotel in Wyoming until she made up her mind? He hit his palm on the steering wheel in frustration.

Tears slid down her cheeks. She knew that she loved him but he had such a commanding presence that her life would never be the same. She and Sarah had made a life for themselves in Wyoming. They could come and go as they pleased. How would Walter possibly fit in?

He must have noticed her tears because he pulled off the side of the rural road. "What's wrong? Does the thought of marrying me make you that unhappy?"

Dana hung her head, wiping her face with the back of her hand. "No, of course not. I just don't know what you would demand of me as your wife."

He reached to hug her. "I wouldn't demand anything, except that you love me and remain in my life. If you and Sarah want to travel, that's fine, too."

"Then you wouldn't mind Sarah living with us in the mansion?"

He laughed. "That house is so big that we might not see her for a week. Besides, she's a darn good cook."

"Much better than I am. Maybe you should marry *her*."

"Don't be silly. We'll talk about this again before I leave." He reached to restart the engine. "Where to, my love. My stomach says I'm hungry."

Dana told him to drive back to the resort. They'd have lunch at the lakeside restaurant where he could take a look at the crime scene. Walter made a U-turn and drove nearly a mile before they approached a T in the road. Pumping the brakes, he swore when the Jeep refused to stop. Sailing past the stop sign, Dana heard the sound of an air horn as the Jeep crashed through a barbed wire fence into a plowed field. Her head made contact with the window frame an instant before she lost consciousness.

When she came to, Walter was holding her in his arms and she felt the sensation of movement.

"Dana!" His voice sounded on the verge of hysteria. "Are you all right?"

Her head throbbed and she couldn't find the words to answer him. A siren wailed in the distance and her world seemed surreal. "What happened?" she finally managed to croak.

"The brakes failed."

Dana groaned and tried to touch her temple.

"You've got a bad bump on your head. The ambulance is coming. A doctor needs to take a look at you."

"But Walter—"

"Please don't argue with me about this. You've probably got a concussion."

Someone behind them said, "Your brake line has a small puncture hole and the fluid leaked out. There's also some damage to the Jeep's front end."

Who was talking? She noticed blood caked on Walter's lower lip.

"A wrecker almost plowed into us," he said. "He'll tow the Jeep to the nearest repair shop."

She suddenly remembered Sarah. If someone had caused the accident, they would go after her as well. "Put me down, Walter. We need to see about Sarah."

"I'll call the sheriff's office and have *them* check on her. You're in no shape to go to anyone's rescue."

For once, she had to agree with him. "Call the resort's security first. Their number's in my wallet."

The siren was earsplitting when it stopped nearby. Moments later Walter stooped to place her gently on the gurney. Why did this have to happen and was Sarah all right?

Chapter Nine

They left the emergency room after four that afternoon. Walter had arranged for a rental car and drove Dana back to the resort. Her head still ached and a purple bruise was darkening her temple. They were both relieved that she had only sustained a mild concussion.

When they reached the motorhome, Sarah was clearly upset when she heard what had happened. Thank heavens Walter was there. But where would he sleep?

He chuckled. "One of the recliners will do. I can't count the times I slept in my patrol car on stakeouts while a deputy kept watch." He tested Dana's chair and found it comfortable enough to sleep in. He then checked the time and announced that he was hungry. They had missed lunch and his stomach was growling loud enough for Jenny to investigate.

"We had planned lunch at the resort restaurant," Dana said, "so why don't we go there for dinner. I want you to see where we found the body."

He frowned. "Are you sure you're up to it? You know

what the doctor said."

She insisted that she was fine but needed to change clothes. When he reluctantly agreed, she and Sarah trooped into the bedroom to rummage through the closet.

Sarah appeared as concerned as Walter. "We don't need to do this tonight."

"I think we do. Walter won't be here long and we need to use his expertise in crime solving."

They dressed quickly, Dana attempting to hide her bruise with makeup before joining the sheriff in the living room. Donning a large floppy hat to further hide her bruise, she grabbed a couple of towels in case Walter decided to wade in the lake. He smiled and offered each woman an arm. "Dinner awaits, ladies. I hope they have a good sirloin on the menu."

The parking lot was empty when they reached the restaurant. Seating themselves on the patio near the lake, Dana pointed out the weeds where the body had been found. Sarah then repeated how she had pursued the diving duck and discovered the body. She also told him about the small, round, orange object stuck in the muddy weeded area.

Walter asked whether anyone had retrieved the ball and offered to look for it the following day. He also wondered if they had come up with other evidence.

"The phoenix button," Dana said. "Did I forget to tell you about it?"

"If it's evidence, you should have turned it over to the sheriff."

Dana said that they had, and told him how the vest and button had been found.

"Is the button old and are you sure it's a woman's vest?"

"Women's clothing buttons to the left, men's to the

right. And the vest is too small for most men."

"So you think the killer's playing games or actually trying to pin the murder on you?"

"He's leaving small clues," Sarah said, "knowing they lead nowhere."

Walter stroked his mustache in thought. "Most killers think they're so smart that they won't get caught, but they get careless and eventually trip themselves up."

From the corner of her eye, Dana noticed a couple seat themselves at the next table. They seemed to be eavesdropping. She was relieved when the waitress approached their own table and conversation came to an end. Walter ordered his steak and Sarah a grilled chicken salad. Dana wasn't hungry but didn't want to worry her companions, so she ordered a soufflé.

"Let's not talk about the case tonight, Walter. Tell us what you've been doing in California."

He said he had been working overtime. He wanted to wrap up all his cases before the new sheriff took office.

"All work and no play?" Sarah asked.

"There'll be plenty of time for play once I retire. Fishing, exploring the Wyoming outback—"

"I didn't know you were a fisherman."

"There are a lot of things you don't know about me, Love."

The couple at the next table pushed back their chairs and left. Dana turned to check them out before they disappeared. The dark-haired woman was of medium height and weight, her balding companion about the same size. Had they ordered dinner and decided to eat inside or were they disappointed that Dana had discontinued the conversation about the murder? It was a lovely, warm evening without a ripple on the lake. She decided they were only there to listen in on how their investigation was progressing. She then remembered the round, orange object in the weeds. Would it still be there the following morning?"

"Walter, I hate to ask, but would you mind retrieving that orange thing in the lake tonight? I'm worried that it won't be there tomorrow."

"Good idea. I noticed that couple eavesdropping. Do you think they're involved?"

"I'm as paranoid as Sarah." She reached across the table to squeeze Sarah's arm. "Who knows why they left, but it certainly was suspicious."

"You haven't eaten, Dana."

"I'll get a doggie bag. Let's check out the restaurant to see if those people are in there."

Walter held the door as they entered the restaurant. A lone elderly man sat a table near the kitchen. No one else was present.

"I thought so," Dana said. "They were here to spy on us." She signaled the waitress and handed her the plate.

"Would you recognize them again?"

"I'm sure I would."

Dana sighed. "Maybe they're in the parking lot out front."

Walter handed the waitress his credit card and hurried to the large bay window. When he returned, he said, "A blue cart just left the lot with golf bags in back."

"If we hurry, we might catch them before they disappear."

"What about the orange object in the lake?"

"I guess I'll have to use a flashlight."

When the waitress returned with his credit card they left.

Dana couldn't imagine Walter wading into the lake after dark, without a wet suit. What had she gotten them all into?

The blue cart was nowhere in sight. A number of side streets crossed the main road and the golf cart must have taken one of them. Dana suggested they return to the motorhome so Walter could change into shorts or a bathing suit.

Back at the RV, Dana searched for a flashlight while Walter changed clothes. Her head still ached and she wondered whether she should follow her friends' advice to lie down. No, she couldn't rest until they solved the murder.

Walter emerged from the bedroom. He was trim and tanned, wearing a red speedo bathing suit. How had he managed to acquire a tan if he had been working overtime? And who had he been tanning with?

He smiled and said, "Tanning bed. I didn't want to arrive at the resort with a farmer's tan."

Before she could protest the dangers of artificial tanning, he insisted they leave for the lake. A few minutes later, they parked at the restaurant and took the path around it.

Sarah waded into the lake with Walter, pointing out the dense patch of weeds where the body had been found. They insisted that Dana remain on the bank holding the towels, where she stood watching as the flashlight clicked on and disappeared in the bulrushes. Concerned there wouldn't be enough light, she watched the orange-red clouds bordering the horizon grow dimmer.

As twilight descended, she heard splashing and Walter's voice. A moment later, Sarah gave a whoop that could be heard in every corner of the resort. They must have found what they were looking for. When the two of them reached shore, Walter handed her a wet, orange golf ball.

"Practice ball," he said. "When we get back to the motorhome, I'll take a closer look at it."

Although she was the only dry one present, Dana shivered in the dwindling light. Was she holding the murder weapon? Or had someone sliced the ball into the lake some time ago?

Walter looked too good in his bathing suit. Was he lying about spending so much time on the job? Or had he been working out to impress her? He wrapped himself in the towel and got behind the wheel. When they reached the motorhome, he said, "Let's go inside and have a look at the ball."

When they had changed clothes, they gathered in the dining nook with Dana, who had already inspected the ball. A small magnifying glass was lying on the table in front of her.

"There's a faint initial on the ball," she said, handing it to Walter. "It looks like a J."

"I think you're right. Remember what I said about smart people making stupid mistakes?"

"But we can't be sure this is the golf ball that killed the Zagori woman."

"Did you notice how large the dimples are? I'll bet my badge it's from a foreign country, but most things are made oversees."

Sarah reached for the ball. "It's still just a cob in the cornfield, Walter."

"But I'll bet the forensics lab can determine its origin."

"You'd better sleep with it in your pocket if you don't want it to disappear," Sarah said. "And keep your gun by your side. Our killer seems to have a knack for picking locks."

Dana touched his arm. "Can forensics match the dimples with the wound on the victim's head?"

"Probably. They're very good at what they do."

Dana suggested they get some sleep. Who knew what would happen the following day. Or during the night, for that matter. The killer must know that Walter was staying with them. Would that discourage him or her from breaking in?

Dana awoke next morning to the smell of coffee. Hearing Sarah's soft snore, she bemoaned the fact that Walter was up so early. Donning her robe and slippers, she opened the pocket door to find him in the kitchen. Setting his mug aside, he greeted her with a hug. When she winced in pain, he asked about her injury.

"I'm fine. What's on today's agenda?"

"This golf ball needs to go to the lab. I'll take it with me when I meet with Sheriff Brandson. In the meantime, we need to get our hands on a lot owner's directory."

Dana didn't think she could acquire a directory before he had to leave. She suggested that he sweet talk the office receptionist into giving him the list. On second thought, the receptionist might still be off sick. Dana didn't think the office manager would cooperate, especially if he had killed Varina Zagori.

She grimaced, remembering the greeting card on the desk signed by the murder victim. How many other men had received similar cards? And had she remembered to tell the investigator about the greeting card? Memory was no longer her strong suit.

"Pennies for your thoughts, Love."

"Just thinking about one of the suspects." She told him about the office manager. "We need to learn his name and talk to his wife."

Walter wiped coffee from his mustache. "What time does the office open?"

"Eight o'clock." She glanced at her watch. "There's time for me to prepare my specialty, blueberry waffles."

"Ah, the lady can cook," he said, lifting his mug. "My cup runneth over."

The pocket door slid open. "Did someone mention waffles?"

Dana sighed and Walter's smile disappeared.

During breakfast they discussed everything that had happened since their arrival at the resort. Walter agreed that discovering the killer was going to be difficult, although not impossible. He wondered how long it would take Sheriff Brandson to solve five murders, unless they were all committed by the same person.

"Sounds more like a metro crime spree," he said. "That usually doesn't happen in a rural area."

Sarah wondered whether the multiple murders were committed to confuse the investigation. She reminded them of the Four Corners murders where four young women had been killed. Walter's arrival had complicated that case but he'd helped to solve a number of others. This one, however, might confound them all.

"I'll ask if the sheriff thinks the cases are connected," Walter said, "although this one seems to stand on its own."

Dana sighed, "There are too many reasons that someone would want to kill Varina. Not only was she promiscuous, she was a convicted blackmailer with a wicked tongue."

"She sounds like a real witch. Not at all like my sweet Dana."

Dana grimaced, wondering why she found it hard to accept his compliments. "Don't forget to verify Varina's cause of death," she said, leaving the dining nook. "I need to get dressed. We have a lot of ground to cover today." She assured Walter that she was up to it.

While the two women were getting dressed, Sarah said, "There's a special meeting of the photography club this afternoon at two o'clock. Why don't we attend while Walter drives to the sheriff's office?"

"Good idea, Sarah. Maybe one of the members will loan us a lot owners' directory."

"We can make a copy on our printer."

"My thoughts exactly. Those women don't seem all that friendly but maybe…

A knock sounded on the sliding door. "You ladies ready to rock and roll?"

Dana ran a comb through her hair and applied lipstick before opening the door. "Ready and impatient to solve this case. Shall we visit the resort office first?" She then told him about the photography club meeting that afternoon.

Sarah joined them and they piled into the rental car with Jenny. The dog seemed happy to be invited along. When they arrived at the office, Walter went in alone. He returned minutes later without the directory. Scowling, he said, "That guy's definitely a suspect. His attitude changed one-eighty when I showed him my badge."

"Did you learn his name, Walter?"

"Yes, Love. It's Jeffrey Dressler."

"Aha," Sarah said from the back seat. "The J on the golf ball."

"Exactly. He refused to hand over a directory, so it's up to you gals to get one this afternoon."

"We also need to find the realtor so I can buy a lot. We'll make it contingent on getting a directory upfront."

Walter protested. "That's a lot of money to spend—"

"Well worth it, and I'll place it back on the market before we leave."

The realtor's office was located around the corner. Walter and Dana went inside where they found a rotund, gray haired woman seated behind an ancient oak desk. Her name plate said Sylvia Koombs. Smiling, she offered them a seat. When Dana asked about the realtor who had driven them around the resort, she said he'd left on vacation.

"But I thought no one was supposed to leave the resort during the murder investigation."

"All I know is that he failed to come to work yesterday morning. I found a note saying he was leaving for a week. That's all I know."

Explaining that she was the company broker, she offered to show them around the resort. Dana said that wasn't necessary. She knew which lot she wanted and gave the broker the number. While Sylvia Koombs was filling out the paperwork, Walter returned to the car to suggest that Sarah take the dog for a walk. When he returned, Dana was writing a check for the entire amount.

"Now," she said, "I'd like that lot owner's directory. I want to know who my neighbors are."

The broker left her desk for another room. They could hear a copy machine churning out pages, then a staple gun fastening them together. When she returned, she said, "You're going to find out sooner or later. The woman who lived next door to your new lot drowned in one of the lakes."

Dana's hand flew to her chest. "I heard she was murdered."

"We've never had a murder take place in the resort and from what I've heard, she suffered a heart attack and drowned."

"Let's go, Dana." Walter took her arm.

The broker said that they couldn't move onto the lot until escrow closed. That usually required two weeks. They thanked the Koombs woman and climbed back in the car. Flipping through the directory, Dana said they no longer needed to attend the photography club meeting. Walter disagreed.

"Listen to every conversation you can while I'm gone. At least I won't have to worry if you're in a group of women."

"I still think a woman killed Varina Zagori."

"You could be right, Love. Be careful and don't leave the clubhouse until I come for you. In the meantime, let's check out your new lot and the ones next to it."

Lot 892 was bare except for a standalone barbeque and inexpensive dining set. However, the lot had a nice view of the lake where the body had been found. It must have been ESP, Dana thought as she re-checked the directory for the location of the Zagori lot next door. She wondered if Varina's widower still lived there. A fifth wheel trailer occupied the space although no car or golf cart were present.

Walter wasted no time investigating. Standing on the edge of Dana's lot, he knelt to view the back of the one next door. He then walked out on the golf course looking for drag marks. None were visible so he assumed the killer had carried the body or lifted it into a golf cart.

"I wonder whether Jerome Zagori plays golf."

"If he does, he's our prime suspect."

"That makes sense. If Varina was leaving him for another man, he might have killed her in a jealous rage."

"Too obvious," Dana said. "The husband is always the prime suspect."

Walter laughed. "People don't think about that when it's a crime of passion. But I'm sure they do if the murder is premeditated."

"It had to have been premeditated if a golf ball was driven into her temple. She must have been lying on the ground when it happened."

Sarah walked over with Jenny. "What about the orange golf ball, Walter? The killer must have gotten rid of the rest."

"Maybe not. Anyone who uses cheap golf balls for practice probably holds onto them." He reached in his pocket to retrieve the ball, encased in a sandwich bag. "The sheriff may have already ordered a thorough inspection of the Zagori's trailer as well as other suspects. And this may not be the murder weapon."

"It will be easier to check out the neighbors once we move onto this lot," Dana said.

Walter gripped her arm. "This is the worst possible place for you to live until the case is solved. What if Zagori's the killer?"

"But what better way to—?"

"You can come here during the day and tell the neighbors you're planning to build an outdoor kitchen or have a canopy erected. You can even plant flowers. But don't accept an invitation to visit inside the Zagori trailer. You could be his next victims."

"He's right, Dana. We'll plant flowers and hope the neighbors come around to see what we're doing. Then they'll tell us about the Zagoris."

A blue golf cart drove by with a couple of lookie-loos. The older couple didn't resemble the people who had eavesdropped at the outdoor restaurant. Dana waved but they were either nearsighted or deliberately ignoring her. Sighing, she realized there were too many residents and not enough time to check them all out.

While Sarah was loading Jenny back into the car, a petite, elderly woman appeared from the other side of the Zagori lot. Her white, short-cropped hair sharply contrasted with her deep tan etched with a multitude of wrinkles. Dana wondered whether she also used a tanning bed.

"You people interested in buying this lot?"

Dana explained that she had already purchased the lot but was waiting for escrow to close.

"I guess it doesn't matter now that the tramp's gone. Nobody ever stayed here longer than a couple of months."

"Really? I wonder why."

"You must be new to the resort."

Dana admitted they were but didn't mention that she and Sarah had discovered the body. She asked the neighbor's name and invited her to sit at the patio table.

"I'm Rosie Darcun and I'm pleased to meet my new neighbors." She explained that she hadn't bothered to meet her neighbors before, because she knew they wouldn't stay.

"Do you know Jerome Zagori?"

"Oh, yes, a nice but stupid man."

"Why?"

"As I said before, his wife was a tramp."

"Do you think he killed her?"

Rosie's laugh was bitter. "I wouldn't blame him if he did. But he's so mild mannered that I doubt he'd kill a slug."

Dana told her that she'd heard the Zagoris were in the process of getting divorced. Did she happen to know who the other party was?

"Hell, it coulda been any number of men as dumb as Jerome."

"Anyone in particular?"

"No, Varina usually hit on older men with money"

"My deceased husband called her a two-bit—"

"I'm sorry. When did he pass?"

"A few months ago." She appeared on the verge of tears. "I was hoping someone would buy my lot so I could move out of here. But now that *she's* gone, I guess I can tolerate the place."

"Tolerate the resort?"

"It's a regular Peyton Place." The old woman invited them over to her lot for a cup of tea.

Once there, Dana looked over Rosie's motorhome. "You have a beautiful rig. A Prevost?"

Rosie nodded. "My husband's pride and joy."

Sarah joined them, still holding Jenny's leash. When she was introduced to Rosie, they were invited into her motorhome. But before they could accept, Walter appeared, shaking his head.

Taking his cue, Dana said, "I'd love to have a cup of tea with you on your patio," Sarah agreed.

Once they were seated at the slate patio table, the old woman leaned to take a look at Dana's bruise. "Did this guy sock you a good one?"

Dana explained about the accident. Looking him over. Rosie decided he could join them. The three of them then sat while their new neighbor prepared their tea.

"Don't trust that woman," Walter whispered. "and stay out of the neighbors' RVs."

"But she's so tiny," Sarah whispered back. "She couldn't have dragged Varina to the lake, and she certainly couldn't carry her."

"It might have been a group effort to get rid of the Zagori woman." Walter looked at his watch. "We can't stay here long. You two will want to change clothes before you attend the club meeting."

"Care to impart some wisdom about what we should ask our fellow club members?"

"I don't think you should ask questions unless it's absolutely necessary. If someone asks how you discovered the body, it will give you an opening to ask about the victim."

They heard something crash inside the motorhome and got to their feet. Sarah rushed to the door to ask what had happened.

"Broke my damn teapot," the old woman said, "and spilled hot tea all over the counter."

Sarah opened the screen door and offered to help with cleanup, but Rosie said help wasn't necessary. Would they mind taking a rain check?

"No problem." Sarah closed the door. "We need to get ready for a club meeting."

Nodding to Dana and Walter, she led the way back to the car. Once they were seated, she said, "You should have seen the coach's interior. That rig must have cost a million dollars."

Dana turned in her seat to stare at Sarah. "From the way she's dressed, she certainly doesn't flaunt her wealth."

Walter laughed. "That exterior paint job must have cost a ton of gold."

"I wonder where she lives and why she's still here. The realtor could sell her lot."

"Next door neighbors make good witnesses, ladies. Sheriff Brandson probably ordered her to stay, just as he did the two of you."

"So you don't think we'd be safe inside Rosie's fancy motorhome?"

"Not unless you have your Smith and Wesson handy. Now that you have your concealed carry permit, you should have it with you at all times."

"And my baseball bat?" Sarah asked, smiling. "That would be hard to explain."

"I'd take it with you in the golf cart just in case."

"I was hoping, Walt, that we'd solve the murder before you leave."

"Walt?" Dana questioned.

"I think I've known him long enough to call him by his nickname. Walter is so formal."

"I agree," he said. "I don't know why Dana insists on calling me Walter."

"I like the name Walter. It means ruler of the army, which I think is quite fitting. It's a Germanic name brought to England by the Normans."

Walter glanced over at her. "You looked that up?"

"Of course I did."

"I'm impressed."

"Don't be...Watch where you're driving. You nearly rear-ended that golf cart."

Sarah leaned between the seats. "It's a blue cart. I wonder if it's the same one we saw at the restaurant."

"We'll soon find out." Walter pulled the car alongside the golf cart and they peered into it. A dark haired woman and balding man were seated inside, with two golf bags in back. As soon as the couple noticed them staring, the cart slowed and negotiated a sharp U-Turn. When it reached the nearest cross street the golf cart turned into it.

"Follow them, Walt. Don't let them get away."

He groaned. "I can't turn the car around until we reach the next intersection."

"Then we'll have to drive up and down all the streets after our club meeting."

"Not a good idea until I get back, Sarah. Concentrate on the meeting."

They pulled into their rented lot a few moments

later.

"Oh, no," Sarah shrieked. "Look what someone did to the motorhome."

Chapter Ten

Walter swore beneath his breath. "Two flat tires. There might be more on the other side."

Dana groaned. "Who could have done this in broad daylight?"

"We need to ask the neighbors and report it to security."

Leaving the car, Walter inspected the damage. When Dana joined him, he said, "Multiple punctures. The tires will have to be replaced."

Sarah arrived with Jenny in tow. The dog sniffed the area and barked.

"What's she trying to tell us, Dana?"

"Probably that she caught the scent of the same person who broke into the motorhome."

"This is getting serious, ladies. I don't think the killer's playing games. Damaging the tires is a warning to stop investigating the murder."

"Shades of déjà vu." Sarah shook her head. "We don't have much luck with motorhomes. Remember what happened to the last ones?"

Dana nodded. A vivid flashback of crashing their first motorhome into a ditch to escape an Arizona killer made her wince. Drug dealers then took out their frustrations on the replacement RV by battering it beyond repair. But when had these tires been vandalized? After they left that morning or during the night?

They needed to check the coach's interior. When the motorhome was unlocked, Walter entered first to check for damage. Everything seemed in order and Dana was relieved they hadn't left the golf ball behind.

Walter called security. They then decided to question the neighbors. The lot to the right of their own was empty so they waved to the neighbor across the street. A slight, wiry little man sat in his lounge chair smoking a cigar. When they approached, his expression said he didn't welcome company.

"I'm sure you noticed the flat tires across the street," Walter said.

"Didn't see a thing. My new glasses aren't ready yet."

Dana and Sarah stood back as Walter squatted next to him. "Have you noticed anyone lingering around the lot lately?"

"Nope. The only people I've seen, other than these women and you, are the groundskeepers. They were there this morning cleaning the lot."

"What about your wife?"

"I'm right here," a woman said from inside the fifth wheel trailer. "We don't pay attention to the neighbors."

Walter thanked them and took each woman's arm as they left. "Call someone to replace the tires before you leave for the meeting. It's going to be a busy afternoon."

The clubhouse was crowded when they arrived. They

found two seats in the back of the room and wondered what all the buzz was about. They didn't have long to wait. The photography club president took the podium and announced a special guest. A former *National Geographic* photographer was there to speak to the group. She then introduced Bob Grosler to a round of applause.

The stout, attractive, middle aged man talked for over an hour about his world travels, then fielded questions about photography in general. Dana asked about bracketing and was satisfied with his answer. Refreshments were served following his talk and Sarah surprised her by waiting until the photographer walked by, smiling at her. Stepping in line behind him, she engaged him in conversation when they reached the refreshment table. Not much taller than Sarah and about the same weight, they resembled a pair of book ends. Dana slipped in next to her and reached for a cookie. In the process, she overheard Sarah invite the photographer to join them.

Once seated, Sarah told him about their slashed tires and asked that he take pictures of them to send to the insurance company. He agreed and couldn't seem to take his eyes from Sarah's face. When they left the clubhouse, she was holding Bob's arm.

Dana silently lamented the fact that they hadn't talked to anyone else. Bob obviously didn't know anything about the murder. Or did he? She asked if he were staying at the resort.

"I'm on vacation and had planned to stay a week, but I might extend my visit." He smiled at Sarah, who seemed in a daze.

"Were you here when the Zagori woman was murdered?"

"As a matter of fact I was. I was out taking pictures of

the ducks on another lake when it happened, so I didn't get a chance to photograph the body."

"You would have taken pictures of the dead woman?"

"I started my career as a police photographer and later served in forensics, so I've taken quite a few pictures of the deceased."

Both women cringed. Sarah then asked if he'd heard people talk about the Zagori woman's death.

"Sure. Gossip seems the main source of entertainment here. I've heard plenty of people talk about the murder victim."

Dana held her breath while he seemed to consider what he should repeat. Before he had a chance to speak, Sarah invited him to their lot for ice tea and the opportunity to get better acquainted. He nodded his acceptance and followed them in his own rented golf cart. Sarah drove and seemed so excited that Dana feared they would have an accident. Hopefully, Bob Grosler would share information about the murder.

Dana hurried into the motorhome to make ice tea while Sarah talked with her new friend. Jenny wanted out, so she attached her leash and decided to walk her down the street. But Jenny would have none of it. Nearly pulling Dana off her feet, the dog made her way to where Sarah and Bob were seated. Sniffing Bob's pants and shoes, she growled and her bark was sharp.

"She probably smells my dog, Barkley," he said. "He's an Australian Shepherd."

When Dana and Jenny returned from their walk, Sarah and her guest were preparing to leave.

"Bob invited me to ride along with him to get his camera equipment," Sarah said. "He also invited me to dinner."

"But—"

She patted Dana's shoulder and whispered, "I'll be

fine."

But would she? Dana didn't think she should ride off with a stranger. Walter would have a fit. *If* Sarah returned, she would invite herself and Walter to make it a foursome for dinner. Urging Jenny into the passenger seat, she followed Bob's golf cart at a distance. If he were renting, he wasn't listed in the directory and she needed to know where they'd gone.

Bob's golf cart turned onto a side street and Dana's cart accelerated. When she reached the street, no other golf cart was in sight. Panicking, she slowed to check out each lot on both sides of the street. Where had Bob's cart disappeared to? She then heard Sarah's laughter near the end of the block. Stepping on the brakes, she hesitated. Should she proceed or turn back? She decided to drive past and wave, saying she was taking Jenny for a ride.

Sarah was nowhere to be seen. Bob's golf cart was parked outside the trailer door, so they must have gone inside. Dana's heart pounded like a kettle drum. What should she do? Pulling a few spaces further down the street she waited, breathing shallowly. If she heard a scream she would rush inside and confront the photographer. Patting her holster, she was reassured that the gun was still hidden inside her waistband. Moments later she heard Sarah's voice, which sounded as though she had left the trailer. Stepping on the accelerator, she goosed the golf cart into a U-turn and drove back toward Bob's lot. He was helping Sarah into his own cart and Dana managed a wide grin and cheery wave as she drove past.

Damnit, Sarah, don't you ever do that again. Dana floorboarded the golf cart although there was a fifteen mile an hour speed limit within the resort. Jenny whined from the passenger seat, obviously frightened by Dana's erratic driving. A speed bump slowed them down but she pulled into their lot well before Bob's cart caught up with her.

Dana was pouring instant tea into tall glasses of ice water when she heard Sarah giggling. Bob must have a well-developed sense of humor to have her friend in constant laughter. She hadn't seen Sarah so happy in ages and prayed that Bob was trustworthy.

Placing three glasses on a tray, she managed to push the screen door open and join them at the patio table. Sarah's expression told her she should make herself scarce, but Dana was determined to check him out.

Putting on her smiley face, she seated herself at the table, which seemed to make Bob edgy. Lifting her glass of tea, she proposed a toast. "To our new friend Bob and our budding friendships." Bob's brief frown told her what she needed to know. He had divide and conquer on his mind. She needed to have a serious talk with Sarah.

"Walter and I would love to have dinner with you two this evening," she said, setting her glass down.

"But, Dana, you need to spend some time alone with Walter. I thought—"

That you want to spend more alone time with Bob. "I'd rather not be talked into marrying him."

Sarah bit her lip, nodding knowingly. She obviously knew that Walter would want to investigate Bob. Maybe even run an NCIC on him.

Dana was relieved to see the rental car pull onto the lot. Walter was scowling when he walked over to them. "I thought you were going to wait for me at the clubhouse. You really had me worried."

Both women apologized before introducing him to Bob. Dana then told him about their encounter. She knew he would withhold any information he'd learned from Sheriff Brandson as long as Grosler was there.

After a brief chat about the photographer's travels, Bob excused himself, claiming a prior commitment. He promised to meet them at the restaurant at six o'clock. Sarah waved when he boarded his cart, but her face crumpled as soon as he was out of sight. "Are you trying to ruin my new relationship?"

"Let's go inside," Walter said. "We need to have a serious talk."

Once they were seated, he said, "Bob Grosler's a phony and you need to stay away from him. He may be a photographer but he didn't work for *National Geographic*."

"How do you know?"

"I've subscribed to the magazine for at least twenty years and I've never heard of Bob Grosler. If he lied about that, he's lying about other things as well."

Tears streamed down Sarah's face. "You don't think he's the killer, do you?"

Walter shook his head. "I warned you both not to go in anyone's RV. You might come out in a body bag."

Sarah changed the subject. "What did you learn from Sheriff Brandson?"

"The Zagori woman suffered a brain injury. A blow to her right temple. Brandson's having the orange ball lab tested and will let me know within the next few days whether it's the murder weapon."

"So she didn't drown?"

"There was some water in her lungs so she must have still been alive when she entered the water."

"Was the time of death established?"

"She died sometime between and nine and eleven o'clock the night before you found her."

"So the killer hid her body until after dark, then either dragged or carried her to the lake."

Sarah said, "The weeds are a ways from shore. That means the body either floated into them or the killer carried Varina into the water to hide her body."

"There's very little wave action in the lake, so I doubt the body would have floated that far."

"That shoots down my theory that it was a woman," Dana said. "Unless she's a weightlifter."

"Varina wasn't very big. I could have carried her, myself."

"That's true, Sarah, but I think that eliminates someone as small as Rosie as the killer."

"Unless she had help," Walter said.

Dana sighed. "With so many enemies in the resort, that's a distinct possibility."

Sarah shifted uneasily in her chair. "What about my dinner date with Bob tonight?"

Walter rose from the recliner to peer from the screen door. "With Dana and me along, we might catch him in another lie that could trip him up. Some men lie to impress women and that may be what Grosler's doing, but I don't trust the man."

Dana joined him. "Jenny doesn't like him either and she's proven to be a good judge of character."

Sarah appeared depressed and Dana turned back to hug her. "The right man will come along. You'll see."

"Not with you two placing him under a microscope." Her friend pushed past Walter to leave the motorhome. Dana followed, watching as Sarah seated herself at the patio table. She obviously wanted privacy, so Dana retreated back inside where the sheriff stood waiting for her. She whispered that she didn't think keeping the dinner date that night was a good idea. Grosler might convince Sarah that he was respectable.

"Not when I get through questioning him," Walter said, closing the motorhome door.

Dana heard a man's voice and peered from a side window. She caught her breath when she noticed Sarah missing. Had Bob Grosler returned?

"She's gone." Dana nearly fell from the steps in her haste to leave the coach. She then spotted Sarah standing at the curb talking to a lanky, older man wearing a western hat and large mustache. She returned inside to watch them through a side window. It wasn't long before they moved to the patio table. Maybe he knew something about the murder. She decided to leave them alone for a while.

Dana sat down heavily in her chair. "Do you think Grosler will show up tonight for dinner?"

"If he's smart he will. I'm glad you didn't introduce me as Sheriff Grayson. That would have put him on guard."

"I hope Sarah didn't say something to him earlier."

"I doubt that she did. She looked too starry-eyed to think about anyone but the photographer."

Dana asked if he had any new thoughts concerning the murder.

"I've got a few but I'd like to mull them over before I talk about them. How about you?"

"We need to talk to the victim's neighbors and think of an excuse to casually interview her husband. Maybe Sarah wouldn't mind whipping up one of her special dishes to take over to him."

"Good idea. I'll drive you two over and wait in the car while you talk to Zagori. My presence might make him uneasy."

"What about the office manager and the vanishing realtor?"

Walter told them he had mentioned the realtor's disappearance to Sheriff Brandson, who ran an NCIC on him. "He came up clean but that doesn't mean he didn't commit the murder." Reaching for her, he pulled her into his arms. "I can only stay a few days. Let's make the most of them."

Managing to wiggle free, she said, "We'll have plenty of time after you retire and this murder case is resolved."

"Worst case scenario is that a crime this complicated can take months. Even years to solve."

She drew back to stare at him. "Are you saying you're not willing to wait?"

"You know I will, although a few more months will be excruciating."

She heard Sarah calling and rushed to the door. Her friend was standing at the foot of the stairs, smiling. "I'd like you to meet one of the Zagoris' neighbors." She turned back toward the patio and they followed.

The lanky man tipped his wide brimmed hat and smiled. "Harry Clasbergan. Pleased to meetcha," he said, extending his hand. "Miss Sarah's been tellin' me about findin' the body."

He resembled the actor Sam Elliot and wasn't wearing a wedding ring. No wonder Sarah's mood had improved. Dana hoped that she hadn't told him that Walter was a lawman. They seated themselves at the table and Dana offered him a glass of tea. He declined but seemed willing to talk about the Zagoris. When Walter asked if he knew the couple well, he shrugged.

"I didn't cotton much to his wife but I shore do like Jerome. He's a fine fellah who got his self tied to a wanton heifer. She wasn't nuthin like this fine filly I'm sittin' next to."

Sarah smiled. "Harry's a retired cattle rancher who lives across the street from the Zagoris."

"I was just out for my afternoon stroll," he said, "when I saw this purdy lady sittin' here all alone."

Walter asked if he made a habit of walking at the same time every day. Harry replied that he sometimes walked as late as midnight, depending on television programming. He lived alone and didn't have much of a daily schedule. Dana asked if he'd been walking the night before the body was found. Harry said he had but that he didn't remember seeing anything unusual. He promised he'd let Walter know if he did.

"You live here full time?"

"Nah, when I sold the ranch I bought four lots in different parts of the country. I wish I had me a travelin' companion." He glanced at Sarah from the corner of his eye.

Dana could swear that Sarah blushed. "Do you think Jerome Zagori killed his wife?"

"He's gentle as a young colt," Harry said. "I'll never understand why he married that maverick heifer."

"Did she hit on you," Sarah asked, knowing that she must have.

Harry's bright blue eyes twinkled. "She did when she found out about my ranch, but I told her to git her tail back home where she belonged. I shoulda turned her over my knee, but she woulda had me tossed in the crossbar hotel."

Dana checked her watch and reluctantly reminded Sarah that their dinner date was within an hour.

Harry wasted no time inviting Sarah to dinner the following evening. Walter intervened, saying, "I hope you understand that women aren't safe in the resort with a killer running loose, so I've advised both Dana and Sarah not to go anywhere without me."

Walter's chaperoning didn't seem to faze Harry. "Shore, the more the better. I'll pick the three of you up tomorrow at six-thirty and we'll do the town."

When he left, Walter said, "He's either the dumbest

man I've met lately, or the smartest."

Dana smiled. "He can't be too dumb if he ran a successful cattle ranch."

"He might have inherited it and run it into the ground."

Sarah sighed. "I wish you two would stop analyzing every man I meet. You know I love cowboys and Harry certainly doesn't have the makings of a killer."

I sure hope you're right, Sarah. Dana opened the motorhome door. "Let's get ready, shall we?"

Chapter Eleven

They waited twenty minutes to order when Bob failed to keep their dinner date. Sarah seemed relieved, but Dana had mixed emotions. There were questions she wanted answered and she knew that Walter was primed to confront him about his photography career. Maybe Grosler had sensed that Walter was in law enforcement. They needed to check out his background on the Internet.

As they were finishing their meals, Harry appeared minus his ten gallon hat. Walter waved him over to their table, and he wasted no time sitting next to Sarah. Sporting a wide grin, he said, "I reckon this is my lucky night. I was hopin' to get better acquainted with you folks, especially Miss Sarah."

She beamed.

"By the way, I have some news that might interest y'all. I heard you bought the lot next to Jerome Zagori. I was talkin' to him a few minutes ago and he said you're welcome to visit him, anytime."

"News travels fast in this place," Dana said.

"Shore does, ma'am. Anyhow, he knows you're investigatin' his wife's murder and he's willin' to tell you anythin' you wanna know."

Dana smiled. "You're a godsend, Harry. Do we need to call or are we welcome to drop by whenever?"

"He's free tonight if you wanna visit."

Dana glanced at Walter, who hesitated before he nodded in the affirmative. "Have you had dinner, Harry?"

"I had me some hen fruit and grits a while ago, but I'll join you for dessert. They serve some good key lime pie."

Harry was rail thin and didn't have to worry about calories. Dana decided that a few added ounces were worth the chance to learn more about Varina Zagori. And she knew that Sarah would never turn down a slice of chocolate cake. Raising her hand, she signaled the waitress, who appeared to have sampled the desserts on a regular basis.

Walter finished first. Setting his empty coffee mug aside, he asked Harry if he knew who the man responsible for the Zagori's planned divorce was.

"It coulda been any number of hombres here at the resort. But I suspect it was the guy from California that owns a gold-plated lot and motorhome. His lot looks like a miniature estate with all the build-outs and greenery."

"His name?" Walter asked in his law enforcement voice, which made Dana cringe.

"Don't recall but you can look him up in the directory. He's located on corner lot eight hundred. I remember that 'cause he's got big gold numbers posted out front."

"Married?"

"Yeah, but his wife's gone a lot."

I wonder if she hired a private detective to track her

husband's whereabouts while she's gone. Dana asked, "Have you formed any opinions about who might have killed Varina Zagori?"

"I have my suspicions, Miss Dana, but I don't wanna tag anybody that might not be guilty."

Walter retrieved a note pad and pen from his shirt pocket. "We'd like to quietly check out everyone who could be involved. No one will know you gave us the information."

Harry glanced about the restaurant, which had emptied with the exception of the waitress, who disappeared into the kitchen. Lowering his voice to just above a whisper, he said, "From what I hear, Varina was involved with a banker whose wife found out about 'em and threatened to kill 'em both. They used to come here every winter but I haven't seen 'em lately. You might check with the office to find out when they left."

"Their names?"

"Ronald and Barbara Smith. I think they're from Tennessee."

"Have you heard anything about the Zagori woman blackmailing anyone?"

"I've heard rumors but nuthin' you could file a claim on." Harry turned to smile at Sarah while Walter scribbled notes.

The waitress appeared at the table to refill coffee cups. Harry held a hand over his, claiming caffeine overload. Dana noticed his hands tremble and wondered why he was nervous. Maybe he had a neurological disease. He appeared to be in his mid to late sixties, so he could have Parkinson's or any number of illnesses responsible for his tremors. It could even be his proximity to Sarah. Dana smiled. He was obviously smitten with her.

Walter returned his notepad to his pocket, suggesting

they pay Jerome Zagori a visit. Harry got to his feet to help Sarah from her chair. Dana approved of him far more than Bob Grosler. Her sixth sense told her Harry wasn't the killer, but she had been wrong about people before.

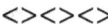

Jerome Zagori's fifth wheel trailer was dimly lit when they pulled onto Dana's lot next door. She noticed flickering light on the shades and assumed he was watching television. Harry accompanied them to make introductions before returning to his own lot across the street.

Once seated, Jerome said he was happy to have nice neighbors moving in next door. Harry must have given him a glowing report. She asked who had previously owned the lot and why it had been sold.

Jerome's expression was one of irritation. "My wife and Gertrude Reaslers didn't get along and I was considering selling our lot when I noticed their's for sale."

"What was the problem?" Walter asked.

"Gertie kept accusing Varina of trying to steal her husband."

"Was she?"

"Of course not. Men were attracted to her because my wife was beautiful."

"But wasn't she planning to divorce you?"

Jerome seemed stunned. "How did you know?"

"Word gets around in a small community. Do you know who she was leaving you for?"

"No. She wouldn't tell me his name."

"Had she filed the papers?"

"She said she had an appointment with a lawyer.

That was the day before she died."

Poor Jerome. I hope he didn't kill his wife in a fit of jealousy. "Were you married long?" Dana asked.

"Three years last January."

"Are you aware that your wife was imprisoned for blackmail?"

"No! You must have her confused with someone else."

"Was her maiden name Whiting?"

"Yes, but—"

"Varina's an unusual name."

"She said she'd been named for her grandmother."

"Is the grandmother still alive?"

Jerome shook his graying head, his handsome face awash with pain. "I'm not sure. I never met her family and Varina didn't talk much about them. I had a feeling they'd had a falling out."

They probably disowned her. Dana asked why they were living in the resort.

"It was Varina's idea. She used to work here in the office."

"As the receptionist?"

He nodded.

"So she was well aware of the people who vacationed here on a regular basis?"

"I believe so."

Walter cleared his throat "Do you have even the vaguest idea who could have killed your wife?"

"So many jealous women hated her. It could have been anyone."

"Any one person more than the rest?"

"Gertie and her husband moved back to Washington last month so I don't think it was her."

Walter asked if he had gone through his wife's belongings to find anything unusual. Jerome shook his head, saying that it was too painful. When Sarah offered to help, he consented to an unspecified time.

"It might help to identify the killer," she said.

Jerome hesitated. "I guess you're right. Maybe you could come back tomorrow."

They agreed. The grieving widower didn't get home from work until 5:45, so they would meet with him then. Sarah offered to bring along a casserole dish so the four of them could share dinner. Jerome seemed grateful and graciously accepted. They left his RV soon after.

Seated in the car, Dana said, "I don't think he killed his wife. His body language says he's telling the truth."

"He actually seems to believe that his wife was a good person," Sarah said. "Varina must have been quite the actress, or he's awfully naïve."

"I wonder why she married Jerome when she had so many men on the string."

"She must have been living in town and driving back and forth to work, Dana. Maybe she couldn't afford a nice trailer so she married someone who could."

"And played the poor, dumb guy for a fool," Walter grumbled from the driver's seat.

Dana sighed. "So do we scratch him off our suspects' list?"

The sheriff said Jerome was still a definite maybe.

When they reached the motorhome and sat to relax, Dana asked if her companions thought Varina had been narcissistic. Walter didn't think so. She'd been using sex as a tool to lure men into compromising situations so she could blackmail them. Married men who feared their wives would divorce them and take half their assets.

"You'd think she would have learned her lesson from her prison sentence," Sarah said. "But maybe she learned from more experienced blackmailers in the slammer, and decided to try a new technique that wouldn't land her back behind bars."

Dana agreed. "Then, there must be a sizeable bank account in her name. She might have hidden the bank statements from her husband somewhere in the trailer."

"Maybe she insisted they pay her in cash. Someone may have followed and killed her to retrieve what he paid." He grinned. "Or maybe she took credit cards."

"Very funny, Walter. I wonder if the Zagoris' trailer was ever broken into to recoup a blackmail payment. On second thought, the killer seems to be a locksmith, so he could have rummaged through the trailer looking for Varina's stash."

"I think she was smarter than that. If she took payments in cash, she must have a safety deposit box in town."

Dana suggested that the money might have been invested in the stock market. "A good place to hide her ill begotten funds, although as volatile as the stock market's been, I doubt she was that much of a gambler."

"Every crook has an Achilles heel," Walter said. "She was smart enough to screw people out of their money, but not as smart as she thought she was. She must have trusted someone she shouldn't."

"A partner in crime, perhaps?"

"Her husband?" Sarah said. "He might have thought she was double crossing him."

"I doubt it. I think it was the man she planned to leave the resort with. He must have gotten greedy. Or disgusted with Varina and decided to take *all* the money."

"Makes sense to me, Dana."

"Then again, she might also have lied about leaving

with another man. If she had acquired a sizeable bank account, she could divorce Jerome and move somewhere else to live as she pleased. Until she found a rich man to marry. Or restart her scheme to replenish her money tree."

Sarah grinned. "You must have a devious mind to think of something like that."

"No more than you, my friend. We've met some devious characters during our travels. Somewhere along the way, those Machiavellian traits can rub off on you."

Walter yawned. "Then I'd better watch my back around you two."

Dana opened an overhead cabinet to retrieve a light blanket to cover him while he slept. She felt sorry for him. He couldn't sleep well in the chair and must be exhausted. She offered her bed, saying that she and Sarah could sleep one night in the living room. Sarah was short enough to sleep on the couch. He declined her offer with a resounding no! It must be a man thing. Dana knew he needed more sleep than he was getting.

Once she and Sarah were settled in their beds, Dana went over all that had happened since their arrival at Paradise Acres. The lighted dial on her watch said half past midnight but she couldn't sleep. She wondered whether Varina's family would attend her funeral or would Jerome decide against a formal service. Maybe the body would be cremated and the ashes scattered across the lake where she died. Dana made a mental note to ask the victim's husband the following day.

She then remembered something Harry had said about Varina hitting on him. He said he didn't have a wife, so had Varina broken her own rules about extorting money from married men? What could she possibly blackmail Harry about? Or was Harry her partner in crime? She prayed that he wasn't. It would break Sarah's heart.

Dana then remembered the conflict in scheduling. Harry had planned to pick them up at six-thirty the following evening, but they promised Jerome to have dinner with him. Memory decline was the worst thing about growing older. She had to write everything down before she forgot. Dana turned over to look at the bedside clock. Two-thirty-four. She must get some sleep.

The next morning, Walter was up before the sun, humming and whistling so loud that it woke Dana from a sound sleep. Would that happen on a regular basis if she married him? He would have to sleep in his own room on another floor. Unable to return to sleep, she lay on her back thinking about her beautiful, deceased sister Georgi, whose husband was responsible for her death. Rob had insisted on separate bedrooms so that he could sneak out at night to sleep with other women. Walter would never cheat on her. She was certain of that, but was she able to cure him of his noisy early morning habits?

Exhausted, she slipped into a near coma and didn't wake again until Sarah tapped her shoulder. Breakfast was ready and they had a lot of investigating to do that day, starting with Bob Grosler and Harry Clasbergan. No one was going to escape their scrutiny.

Chapter Twelve

Dana booted up the computer immediately after breakfast to research Grosler's background. He wasn't listed on any of the locator sites and she concluded that his name was an alias. How were they going to track him down? Maybe the photography club president knew who he actually was? Did photographers have pseudonyms like writers?

She next typed in Harry Clasbergan's name. He was listed as living in rural Texas with his wife, Martha, and four daughters. His offspring must all be living on their own since he sold the ranch. He had probably divided the proceeds of the ranch sale among them, leaving himself enough money to buy four RV lots.

But what about his wife? Was she still living? When she clicked on the criminal record section and paid the fee, Harry turned up clean. Sighing with relief, she relayed her findings to Walter and Sarah.

"Looks like Grosler's our man, if we can find him. He's probably halfway to Tahiti by now."

"I wonder what connection he had to Varina Zagori.

Was he a partner in crime or one of her victims?" Sarah said. "He didn't seem rich enough to blackmail, so he must have been in cahoots with her."

Dana smiled to herself, thinking how well-suited Sarah was to the cowboy. They spoke the same language. She hoped he was no longer married. "We need to contact Harry about the conflict in scheduling. Why don't we invite him to join us for dinner at Jerome's place tonight? We can have dinner on the patio."

Sarah agreed but Walter wasn't so sure. "Too many cooks can spoil the stew, as my mother used to say. The more people involved, the more complicated things can get. Harry served his purpose by introducing us to the murder victim's husband."

Turning to Sarah, he said, "Why don't you apologize for the mistake and reschedule for tomorrow night with Harry?"

Sarah hesitantly agreed. Spending time with Harry had obviously taken precedence over solving the murder. That worried Dana. Sarah had been without male companionship for far too long, but it shouldn't interfere with the problem at hand.

Once they left the motorhome and were seated in the car, Sarah directed Walter to the Grosler lot. Bob's golf cart was parked outside his door but no one answered when Walter knocked.

"He's probably hiding, pretending not to be at home."

As they turned to leave, a neighbor walked over to tell them that Grosler had been taken to the hospital in an ambulance the previous evening.

"Sick?" Walter questioned.

"Someone bashed him over the head and he was bleeding badly."

"No wonder he didn't show up for dinner," Sarah

said.

Walter puckered his lips in thought. "Head wounds bleed profusely, if the blow doesn't kill the victim."

Sarah smiled. "That means he's probably not guilty."

"Maybe. Let's make a trip to the hospital to see how he's doing."

The neighbor shrugged and returned home as they boarded the car. Dana wondered aloud if Bob Grosler hit himself on the head to divert suspicion.

"As far as I know, he wasn't under suspicion unless one of the investigators has been questioning him. I'd better give Steve a call."

Dana didn't ask, but her question was answered when she heard Walter ask for Sheriff Brandson. At least they were on a first name basis. When he clicked off, he said that Grosler claimed his attacker hit him when he left his golf cart to unlock the trailer door. A deputy had questioned him at the hospital.

Sarah leaned over the console. "Does he believe Bob's story."

"Sheriff Brandson is reserving his opinion until further investigation. I personally agree with Dana's assumption that he managed to do it himself."

Sarah's expression was doubtful.

"By the way, the orange golf ball *is* the murder weapon. Good job, ladies."

"Yes!" Sarah said. "I knew it was."

"Now all we need to know is who hit the ball that killed her. And why."

"Whoever tried to bury the murder weapon in the mud must have long arms because even Dana couldn't reach it."

"They could have dived beneath the surface like one of your ducks."

"After dark, Walt? How could they see what they

were doing?"

"The ball could have been placed at the end of a hollow tube and rammed into the mud."

"That would mean the murder was premeditated and carefully planned."

"I agree, but was the ball buried *before* the body was dumped in the water, or after?"

Dana thought that the killer would first want to get rid of the murder weapon and wait until the wee hours of the morning to get rid of the body. But Walter disagreed. He reminded them that the victim had water in her lungs, which meant she was still alive when placed in the water. She could have remained alive and unconscious with a brain hemorrhage for a few hours or even suffered a stroke, but she had to have been in the lake not long after the attack.

"If she were still alive," Dana said, "the killer must have held her head under water until she drowned."

"A good possibility. We need to ask Varina's husband when he reported her missing. We know he returns home promptly at 5:45 each afternoon. Was his wife usually there to greet him? If not, when did he realize something was wrong?"

"Don't forget the vest with the phoenix button, Walt. I'm sure that ties in somehow with the murder. But who's planting clues or trying to throw us off track? The killer or someone who's afraid to come forward to tell what happened?"

Walter sighed as he turned the key in the ignition. "I'm afraid time's not on our side. I only have two days of my leave left and I'm afraid to abandon you two. Maybe I can talk Sheriff Brandson into allowing you to disappear for a while."

Dana's chin jutted forward. "Don't worry about us. We can take care of ourselves."

"So you've said before, but this case is different. It's like chasing a ghost and we still don't know its gender. Or was it a group effort for that matter. I feel like Don Quixote tilting at windmills."

Sarah agreed. "Too many suspects and not enough time."

"Let's visit Grosler in the hospital and see what he has to say about his attacker."

The trip lasted twenty minutes and they found a space in the ER parking lot. Walter had called during the drive to learn Grosler's room number. He punched in the third floor button when they boarded the elevator. When they reached his room, Grosler's door was open, his head bandaged like a beehive. He was sitting up in bed when they entered his room.

"Sarah," he said as soon as he noticed her. Reaching out, he took her hands and squeezed them. "I'm sorry I missed our dinner."

Sarah pulled away when Walter told him it was an official visit, not a personal one. He then launched his interrogation. Grosler stammered several times when questioned about the attack.

"I didn't see who it was. All I know is that someone hit me on the back of the head while I was unlocking my trailer door. I don't remember anything else until I came to in the hospital."

"Daylight or dark?"

"I-I don't remember. It must have still been daylight because I was planning to shower and dress for dinner when it happened."

Walter asked why someone would attack him. Did he have an enemy in the resort? Grosler winced when he shook his head saying he knew few people and had never stayed there before.

"Did your attacker take anything, like your wallet?"

"No, and that's strange. The nurse said everything I asked about was still in my pants pockets, including my wallet."

"What about your fifth wheel? Had you unlocked the door before the attack?"

"No, I was fumbling in my pockets for the key, thinking about Sarah at the time, so I wasn't conscious of any movement." He smiled at Sarah, who turned away.

Walter said he had one last question and wanted a straight answer. "Why did you lie about working for *National Geographic*?"

Grosler sighed heavily. "I have traveled the world freelancing for lesser magazines and felt that my work was as good as anything published in their magazine. But they wouldn't buy my work. I know it was a stupid lie but it impresses people who don't bother to check. It also gets me speaking engagements and—"

"The admiration of women," Walter finished for him.

Grosler ducked his head. "That too. I noticed Sarah in the audience while I was speaking and wanted to meet her. So I was glad that she thought I was a world class photographer."

"Not the best way to start a relationship," Sarah said.

He winced when he nodded his agreement. "Can you forgive me?"

Sarah shrugged but said nothing more.

Walter ended the conversation with "Get well. We'll talk later." He then steered the women into the hall.

In the elevator Walter asked if Sarah was still interested in Grosler. She said she could no longer trust him and would rather spend time with Harry. Dana sighed inwardly, happy with Sarah's decision.

"Now what, Love?" They stood in the parking lot

watching Walter unlock the car "Any ideas where we should go next?"

"Grocery store to gather ingredients for tonight's special dinner," Sarah said. "I know you don't want Harry to join us, but I plan to dazzle him with my cooking. He can take the hint to leave after dinner, if you think he shouldn't be around."

"Fair enough."

That evening at dinner Jerome seemed unusually nervous. Dana wondered why he had consented to answer questions, if he had something to hide. While she and Sarah cleared the patio table, the three men had their heads together discussing something she was unable to hear. Walter would tell her later but she was curious about the subject of their conversation. When the dishes had been washed in Jerome's kitchen and put away, they returned to the patio.

Looking up, Walter said, "Jerome has consented to allow us to search his trailer for clues. Sarah, why don't you keep Harry company out here while Dana and I do a quick inspection?"

Sarah seemed happy to comply and seated herself close to Harry. Dana was uneasy about going through the dead woman's personal affects, wondering whether Jerome had already done so. After a brief search of the small bathroom closet, they moved on to the bedroom dresser drawers. The contents didn't provide any clues so Walter pulled out the drawers to inspect the undersides of each one. In the last drawer he discovered a key taped to the bottom. Turning it over, he inspected the key carefully.

"Doesn't appear to be a bank deposit key. It looks

more like one that opens a locker."

Jerome's face darkened. "My wife didn't go to a gym. She jogged around the resort to stay in shape."

"Mind if I take this?" Walter asked. "I'll turn it over to Sheriff Brandson."

Jerome's hands raised in a *why not* gesture. "I have nothing to hide."

Dana remembered the vest. "Did your wife own a gray vest with a large phoenix rising button?"

He shook his head. "She didn't like the color gray. She always wore colors like reds, yellows, oranges and bright blues and greens."

Probably to attract attention to herself. "Are you absolutely sure?"

"Yes, I bought her a pretty gray sweater for her birthday and she refused to wear it. She said it made her look old."

"Did she return it?"

"Oh, yeah. She came back from the store with an armload of clothes to replace the sweater."

I'm sure she had plenty of blackmail money to pay for them. "So your wife was a clothes horse?"

"You saw the closet. I barely have room to hang a few of my own clothes."

"Mind if I take another look?"

His sweeping arm gave her permission.

While she felt the pockets of Varina's clothing and inspected the contents of her purses, Walter rummaged through the kitchen cabinets. Dana then thought to look more closely in the bathroom closet. A box of sanitary pads sat on the floor in the back and she pulled it out to inspect. Under the pads was a thick, legal-sized envelope sealed with transparent tape. When she showed it to Walter, he asked Jerome to open the envelope. Inside was a thick stack of one hundred dollar bills.

"We need to turn this money over to the sheriff as evidence," Water said.

Jerome seemed in shock. "I have no idea where that came from. Varina must have saved part of her earnings for years."

"Blackmail money," Walter said. "Do you have a laptop? We have something to show you."

While Jerome pulled the laptop from a desk drawer, Walter asked about the night Varina disappeared. Was she home when he arrived? The answer was no. Was that unusual? Placing the laptop on the desk, Jerome said his wife loved people and sometimes forgot to watch the time, so it wasn't unusual for her not to be at home to greet him.

"When did you report her missing?"

Jerome bit his lip. "I searched the resort first to find our golf cart but I couldn't find it. The police later found it parked between two trees near the lake near where her body was. When I couldn't find Varina or the cart I was worried and phoned security. They called the sheriff's office."

Dana touched his arm. "I'm so sorry. I hate to show you what I discovered online." She sat at the desk and booted up the computer to show Jerome his wife's criminal record.

Chapter Thirteen

Dana was worried about Jerome "He took his wife's criminal record badly. I hope he doesn't do something desperate."

Walter reached to pat her arm. "I find it hard to believe that he didn't have some inkling of what she was up to. Somebody must have tried to warn him."

Sarah reminded them that love is blind. "Varina must have had the poor man hypnotized." She rose from her recliner to renew their supply of tea. They had brainstormed for more than an hour since returning to the motorhome, but still hadn't come up with any answers.

Walter felt they had whittled down their list of probable suspects but still needed to investigate the wealthy Californian in lot 800. Dana moved to the small desk to boot her laptop while Walter ran his finger down the owners' directory.

"I found them: Stan and Alberta Rosenbine of San Francisco. I think we should pay them a visit tomorrow morning."

The women agreed. "The Rosenbines are from your own territory, Walt. That should make it easier, although they'll probably wonder what you're doing here."

"The murder victim had been incarcerated at the California Women's Institution. That gives me reason enough to ask questions."

Dana gasped. "Isn't that one of the women's prisons where nearly a hundred-fifty prisoners claimed to have been involuntarily sterilized?"

"As I recall, they all signed releases for exploratory surgery for cancer and other ailments, not to have their reproductive organs removed or tied off."

"I wonder if Varina was one of them."

"If she was, it could explain her promiscuity."

"It could also explain her disregard for other people."

Sarah handed them each a refilled cup of tea. "That doesn't excuse her actions. She was a blackmailer before she went to prison, and I'm sure she learned a few things while she was there."

Walter drank half his tea before setting it aside. "I'll check her records when I return to work. Maybe I can find a clue buried in her past."

"The sooner the better, Walt. I'm more than ready to leave for home. I feel like a prisoner trapped in Paradise, which is long way from utopia."

Sarah's remarks surprised Dana. "What about Harry?"

"If he wants to see me, he can come to Wyoming. With my luck, he'll turn out to be the killer's sidekick. I guess I'm just getting paranoid about men. Especially those in the resort."

"I can't say I blame you, but you can't give up hope."

Walter suggested they all get a good night's sleep. They would interview the Rosenbines the following morning and then attempt to locate the vanishing realtor. There was also the office manager to investigate. Hopefully they could also talk to his wife.

Dana yawned her way to bed but couldn't fall asleep. Insomnia was becoming a habit. When she finally dozed off, she found herself in a cell with a doctor standing over her, holding a foot long hypodermic needle. Screaming, she awoke trembling. Fortunately, she didn't wake Sarah and Walter didn't mention hearing her the following morning. But he *was* unusually grumpy. Sleeping in the chair had to be wearing him out.

After breakfast Jenny's needs were met before they left the RV. Dana hoped Alberta Rosenbine wasn't home. It would be much easier questioning her husband without her present.

As they approached the corner lot, a blond woman driving a Mercedes backed onto the street in the direction of the main gate. It must have been Alberta Rosenbine.

A squat, seventyish man answered the door in his white cashmere robe. Displaying his badge, the sheriff asked to speak to Stanley Rosenbine. When the man hesitated, he was told he was investigating Varina Zagori's death.

"What's that got to do with me?"

"Witnesses have said that you were involved with her."

Rosenbine stuck his head out the door, looking in both directions before he invited them inside. He then asked why the women were along. When told they had discovered the body, he motioned them to be seated in his elaborately decorated coach.

"How long did you know the deceased?" Walter asked.

"For some time. We met at the office while Varina was the receptionist. I later heard she had married while my wife and I were in Vancouver."

"When did you start seeing her socially."

Rosenbine coughed and tugged his robe tighter about him. "During our second winter here two years ago. My wife was visiting her sister in New Hampshire when I met Varina at the tennis courts. She was friendly, attractive... and one thing led to another."

"Did she blackmail you, threatening to tell your wife about your affair."

"No, but she convinced me to leave my wife and meet her in Hawaii."

"When was that?"

"A couple of days before she died."

"Had you talked to your wife about a divorce?"

"No, I couldn't go through with it, but I hadn't told Varina that yet."

"So your wife doesn't know?"

He sighed. "I hope not. I love my wife but she travels a lot for her cosmetics company. And I get lonely."

Walter asked if an investigator from the sheriff's office had questioned him. Rosenbine said he hadn't talked to anyone about the death. He had hoped no one knew, and asked how the three of them had heard about the affair. Told it wasn't common knowledge, he seemed to relax and answer the rest of Walter's questions.

When they left, no one spoke until they reached their own motorhome. Dana then made them ice tea and they sat in the dining nook talking in hushed tones.

When asked, Dana said she thought Rosenbine had been telling the truth and that he was experiencing extreme guilt pangs. Sarah said she had come to the same conclusion, although Walter refused to cross him off his suspects' list.

"I do think he's lying about Varina blackmailing him, Walt. He must have told her he wasn't leaving his wife and she threatened to expose him."

Walter shook his head. "Somebody should tell his wife to stay home more often. You have to feel sorry for an abandoned spouse."

"Not if he killed his mistress."

"When you asked if he knew Varina had been in prison, I thought he would swallow his tongue."

Dana agreed. "I think he was genuinely disgusted with himself for getting involved with her. But was he angry enough to kill her if she actually tried to blackmail him?

"Walt, a man with that much money is used to getting his own way. I doubt that he would allow someone like Varina to threaten him. Even if he *was* sleeping with her."

"If he's a bully, it could explain why his wife's away so often," Dana said.

Walter slid from the nook. "I don't have much time left here. I think we should check on the illusive realtor."

The groundskeepers were mowing the golf course opposite them, the noise making it difficult to hear. Motioning them outside, he unlocked the car and beckoned them into it. When they reached the realty office, they noticed a closed sign on the door. Dana checked her watch, remarking that it was after ten o'clock. Realtors must keep bankers' hours.

They decided the broker was showing a prospective buyer resort lots, if her employee was still missing. They would check back later. Dana copied the phone number listed on the window, hoping it was a cell phone.

"That leaves the office manager," Walter said as he

135

ushered them back to the car. "I'm not quite sure how to approach him if the receptionist is there."

Dana suggested that he go in alone and flirt with the receptionist. "You can say that she's a lot nicer than Varina. Maybe she'll open up about her."

Walter smiled. "You are a devious woman, Love. It just might work if the manager doesn't stick his nose into the conversation."

"Sarah and I can distract him by telling him we're concerned about our safety, and ask what he thinks we can do to protect ourselves. We'll ask questions until he throws us out."

"Good idea. But don't say anything about the Zagori woman. We don't want to make him suspicious. Just keep your eyes open for photographs or other evidence."

"Safety in numbers." Dana patted her concealed holster. "We'll keep him occupied as long as possible."

"Be careful. Don't drag your questions out too long. Ten minutes should be sufficient. If the receptionist doesn't take the bait, I'll be waiting here in the car."

Dana and Sarah entered the office first. The petite, middle aged receptionist was busy at her computer and barely glanced at them when they approached the counter. Dana asked for the manager and the receptionist buzzed him on the intercom. When he appeared a few moments later, Dana said they would like to speak with him privately.

Sighing, he led them back to his office, which was similar in size to the one they just left, although more comfortably furnished. Two chairs sat before his impressive desk and they took them after covertly scanning the room for incriminating evidence. Several framed pictures sat on his desk, their backs to visitors, surrounded by several tall stacks of documents. He appeared disgruntled that his work had been interrupted.

Folding his hands on the desk, he asked, "What specifically would you like to know?"

"We're worried about our safety here in the resort."

"Why? There are several deputies patrolling the grounds."

Dana then told him about her punctured tires.

"I've had reports of kids vandalizing RVs. I'll look into it. Anything else?"

"We'd like a resort map indicating the laundry and sports facilities."

He rummaged in a lower drawer of his desk and handed her a map. Dana was disappointed that he didn't leave the room long enough for them to briefly turn the photographs around.

"Is that all?"

She asked about the groundskeepers, social activities, and anything else that came to mind. When she ran out of questions, Sarah had some of her own. Had ten minutes gone by? She was hesitant to look at her watch. She knew he was impatient to return to work and didn't want to make him suspicious, so she thanked him and they left. Walter was still standing at the counter when they walked by, ignoring him. Moments later, he met them at the car.

"I hope you don't mind that I invited the receptionist to lunch at the restaurant. She was too busy to answer questions but I think she'll open up about the Zagori woman once she leaves the office. You two can take a nearby table and eavesdrop."

"Great idea, Walt. I hope she doesn't invite you back to her place after work."

"I hope she does, if she has valuable information about the case."

I suggested flirting with her, not having an affair.

"Does she know you're in law enforcement?"

"No, I didn't tell her." He peered at her curiously. "You're not jealous, are you?"

"Of course not. What time is your lunch date?"

"Half an hour. I'll pick her up first and you two can arrive a few minutes later in the golf cart."

Sarah patted his shoulder. "Good plan. That will give me time to find my palm recorder."

"Not a good idea. She might spot it and clam up."

"If you're depending on our memories, I'm afraid you're out of luck."

He grinned. "No problem. I have a pen recorder in my shirt pocket."

Dana thought back to the first time she had seen Walter Grayson, an experienced police dog trainer recently elected sheriff. He had not only grown more experienced, but attractive as well.

"I nearly forgot," he said. "The repair shop called while I was in the office. Your Jeep is ready for pick up. Let's plan on driving there after lunch."

Dana was relieved. She disliked the rental car and wanted to feel in command again behind the wheel. It wasn't that she resented Walter sitting in the driver's seat. She disliked the role of passenger and not having control over her own destiny.

The receptionist must not have liked dining al fresco because they were sitting near the windows in the restaurant when Dana and Sarah arrived. It was still early for luncheon diners so they had their choice of tables. Sitting quietly behind the receptionist, they listened to the conversation.

The receptionist was saying, "I took the job when

Varina quit to marry Jerome. I thought it was strange that she choose such a quiet man when her escorts had all been well-to-do gentlemen."

"Did you know her well?"

She shrugged but didn't answer.

"Were you friends?"

"I wouldn't call us friends. She didn't get along well with women."

"Why was that?"

"She was more interested in men. She would go out of her way to please them. Not so with women."

"The two of you work together?"

"For about a month while she trained me for the job."

"Was she a good person or are the rumors I've heard about her true?"

"Rumors?"

"About her character?"

"Why are you asking all these questions?"

Walter hesitated. "I'm investigating her murder."

"Why didn't you say so? I thought that you were—"

"Interested in you?" Walter apologized, telling her she was an attractive woman but that he was engaged to be married.

Her shoulders slumped and her fork clattered to her plate.

You didn't handle that well, Walter. Now she won't tell you anything. Dana watched as he reached across the table to place his hand over hers. Jerking free, she left her chair and hurried from the restaurant.

"I hope she doesn't tell her boss," Sarah said.

Walter looked across the room into Dana's eyes. "It's all right," she mouthed. She was glad that he wasn't skilled at charming women. They would have to figure out another way to get the information they needed.

Tomorrow was his last day in Paradise, so they'd better make the best of it.

Chapter Fourteen

They dropped off the rental car on their way back from the repair shop. Dana insisted on driving the Jeep, forcing Walter to occupy the passenger seat. During the drive back to the resort she asked what the mechanic had said about the punctured brake line, and wondered whether the damage had been done deliberately.

"He's not sure. That's why I'm worried about you two. If it were to happen again, you could be seriously injured. And if Sheriff Brandson won't allow you to leave, I suggest you have the dog sleep in the Jeep at night or make her bed next to the back bumper."

"I'm afraid Jenny would bark at anyone who passes by. We could rig up a spotlight and park the Jeep beside the motorhome."

"Good idea, but that's not foolproof."

"If you tell the sheriff we're in danger, he'll insist on taking us in for protective custody."

"Better than losing your lives. Remember your punctured tires? That was a definite warning to stop investigating the murder."

"Was the brake line puncture deliberate?"

"I'm afraid so. You can theorize all you want about the killer, but you need to leave the investigation to the authorities." He stared sternly at them both. "How do you expect me to return home and wrap up my job while I'm worried about you?"

Dana knew Walter was right but felt they were close to solving the crime. It had to be someone they'd met at the resort, who was constantly watching them.

"We won't question anyone," Dana said. "But if we overhear something important, we'll report it to the sheriff."

He warned them not to make any unnecessary trips to town and to drive around the resort first to test the brakes. He would check the golf cart before he left, and reminded Dana to never leave the motorhome without her concealed weapon.

"Let's check again on the missing realtor before we reach your lot."

Dana pulled into a reality office parking lot. This time the open sign was prominently displayed on the door. Sylvia Koombs was seated behind her desk and gave them a cheery wave while she talked to someone on the phone. When she hung up, they asked about the vacationing realtor.

"Haven't heard a word from Paul. If he's not back by tomorrow, he'll be looking for another job."

"Has he done this before?" Walter asked.

"Never. He's been my most dependable realtor."

"Have you checked with the police or the hospitals?"

No, but I talked to his wife, Lacey. She hasn't heard from him either."

"She's still here in the resort?" Dana was stunned.

The broker nodded yes, a disgusted expression on her face. "Oh, by the way, Missus Logan, escrow should close on your lot next week."

*So soon? I'm not ready to move over there next to
the victim's lot.* Dana and Walter exchanged glances
and she knew what he was thinking. They were placing
themselves in even more danger.

Back in the Jeep, Walter said, "We need to pay the
realtor's wife a visit. I didn't ask the broker where
the woman lives because we can look her up in the
directory. I think I should go alone in case the killer's
watching."

"But—"

"Investigate all you want on the computer and
phone, but don't let anyone see you visiting possible
witnesses."

Both women agreed but Dana noticed doubt in
Walter's eyes. He obviously didn't believe that they
wouldn't follow up on their suspicions once he was
gone.

Jenny was barking when they arrived back at the
motorhome. They should have taken her along. Sarah
snapped on her leash and took the dog for a walk while
Dana looked up the realtor's lot in the directory. Walter
left to visit Lacey Gates before Sarah returned with
Harry. Dana wasn't sure they could trust the cowboy,
but Sarah was convinced he was harmless.

Sarah invited him into the coach and offered him
something to drink. Seated on the couch, he asked how
the investigation was going. Dana gave Sarah a look
and told Harry they had abandoned the case because it
had become too dangerous.

Harry's face fell. "Aw shucks. I was gonna offer to
help."

A cold chill ran down Dana's spine. Was he the killer
or just a lonely old man?"

"I was on my way over here when I met up with my

gal, Sarah. I was gonna tell you that Bob came home from the hospital this mornin'. He's still got a bandage on the back of his head but he seems bright-eyed and bushy-tailed."

You're a regular walking newspaper, Harry. "Glad to hear it," Dana said. "I wonder why someone would attack him."

"I can't imagine 'less he knows somethin' about the murder."

"He told us that he's never been here before. Was he telling the truth?"

"I never saw him until almost two weeks ago. I can ask why he came here, if you want."

"Only to satisfy our curiosity, Harry. Remember we're off the case."

"I'd like to know myself. He's a strange duck who goes around tellin' ever'body he's a famous photographer."

"We know," Sarah said, moving closer to him. "How would you like to have dinner with us tonight?"

Dana gasped. She then remembered that Walter would still be in residence.

"I shore would, little lady. Last night's home cooked meal at Jerome's place was the best I'd had since my wife Martha died." He appeared genuinely grief stricken. Sarah hugged him and murmured she was sorry.

Maybe Harry actually was just a lonely widower seeking companionship. Dana knew she had become too suspicious. "We'd be pleased to have you join us tonight."

Harry left to talk to Bob Grosler minutes before Walter returned from talking to the realtor's wife. Seating himself in Dana's recliner, he said Lacey Gates had reported her husband missing that morning. An investigator from the sheriff's office was due to arrive any moment.

Dana sat in the chair next to him. "So she had no inkling that he was about to leave?"

"None. She said he dressed for work that morning and all he took was his brief case."

"No overnight bag or change of clothes?"

"Not according to his wife. She said he left a little early, saying he had a client waiting at the office. She didn't suspect otherwise."

"You don't suppose he's the killer and thought the sheriff was on to him?"

"Could be. I asked if she knew Varina Zagori and was told they had visited with the Zagoris on several occasions after her husband sold them their lot."

"How did she feel about Varina?"

"She didn't like her although they both like Jerome."

"Did she suspect anything going on between her husband and Varina?"

"She didn't say but I got that feeling. I was surprised she told me as much as she did. I then realized she thought I had arrived to take the missing person's report."

"Good thing you left when you did, Walter. I wonder if Lacey Gates disliked Varina enough to kill her."

"And do away with her husband as well," Sarah said.

"A good possibility, ladies. What's for lunch?"

"Leftovers from last night's dinner." Dana rushed to the refrigerator while Sarah told him about Harry's visit. She asked his opinion of the aging cattleman.

"He seems harmless enough but I wouldn't trust him alone with you. I'm afraid Dana's going to have play chaperone after I'm gone."

"Chaperone?" Sarah's mouth flew open. "I'm sixty years old. I certainly don't need—?"

"Just until the killer's arrested."

Dana said, "Harry seems to know what everyone in the resort is doing."

"A good subterfuge if he's the killer."

"He's a dear, sweet man," Sarah countered. "He couldn't possibly have murdered Varina."

"What if he committed a mercy killing to protect his friend Jerome?"

"Mercy killing?"

"If he does know what goes on in the resort, he also knows the men Varina had affairs with and, maybe, who she blackmailed. He might have considered killing her as a compassionate act."

Sarah sat down heavily in the nearest chair. "Oh, dear, I hope that's not true."

"I'd encourage him to talk about the other lot owners, but be prepared to defend yourselves if he realizes he's said too much." Walter rose from the chair to pull Dana to her feet. "And you, Love, must keep your gun handy at all times. I know it's not comfortable wearing that concealed holster, but it's necessary."

She sighed. "Why can't Sarah and I take a vacation without getting embroiled in at least one murder?"

"We're murder magnets," Sarah reminded her as she set the table.

"Let's drive over to your new lot after lunch and putter around until another curious neighbor shows up."

"But, Walter, you said to leave this case up to the authorities."

"After I leave when there's no one here to protect you." He asked if they had a tape measure. Dana took one from a drawer and handed it to him. "What's this for?"

"We're going to pretend to take measurements of your lot. That ought to stir up someone's curiosity."

"Including Harry and his crabby little neighbor Rosie? I'm sure Harry has already spread the word by now that we're no longer investigating the murder."

"That's good. It may prevent further vandalism and possibly save your lives."

They measured the lot in every possible direction, recording the measurements in Walter's pocket notebook, but no one came to inquire what they were doing. Jerome was still at work and Harry wasn't around. As they prepared to leave, Rosie walked over to investigate. Her short gray hair was hidden beneath a light blue baseball cap, which matched her eyes. The overalls she was wearing were grass stained at the knees and so small that they must have been purchased in a boy's clothing department. She couldn't have stood taller than four feet ten inches in her wedgies. Technically she was a dwarf. And dwarfs weren't known for committing crimes.

"You folks planning to build on your lot?"

"We're considering it. What have *you* been up to?"

"Flower gardening as you can see. A trowel handle protruded from her overalls' pocket and she wore a stained pair of gloves."

"Anything interesting happen around here lately?" Sarah asked.

"Just the usual RV hopping, booze parties, church socials..."

"You haven't by chance heard what happened to the realtor, Paul Gates, have you?"

"I heard he's missing. He probably took off with some young chick and will return in a few days claiming temporary amnesia."

"Has he done that before?"

"Not to my knowledge, but nothing that happens here surprises me."

"You know most people in the resort?" Sarah said.

"Oh, sure, they come and go but I know the old-timers."

"Like Harry across the street?"

"Nice man but a little too nosey for me. He's always asking questions."

"A sign of intelligence," Walter said. "Has he ever been in trouble?"

"No, why do you ask? Oh, you think he might have killed Varina?" Rosie laughed. "He doesn't have it in him. He loves women too much. He has lady friends all over the resort. There's gonna be a cat fight one of these days."

Sarah's face fell and Dana feared she would cry.

"Nice talking to you," Dana said, glancing at her watch. "We need to go."

"Let me know when you're moving in and we'll have a lot warming party."

They waved goodbye from the Jeep and Sarah drove them back to the motorhome over the speed limit. "Good thing security didn't catch you flying," Walter said. "They'd probably lock you in the clubhouse."

"Better than the hoosegow."

"Harry's a lonely old man, Sarah. You can't blame him for making friends."

"All of them women?"

Walter opened the Jeep's back door. "Maybe he had a harem in a former life."

Dana glared at him a second before she noticed movement in her peripheral vision. Bob Grosler had parked his golf cart on the street and walked back to their lot. Spotting Sarah behind the wheel, he gave her a big smile and opened the door for her. Sarah hesitated before accepting his hand and leaving the driver's seat.

"How's your head?" she asked.

"Not bad. I missed seeing you and thought we might have that dinner I missed when I was in the hospital."

"I'm really not feeling well, Bob. May I take a rain check?"

"Sure, but can I talk to you privately before you go inside?"

Sarah turned to glance at Dana who still occupied the passenger seat. When she nodded her approval, Sarah led him to the patio table. Dana and Walter went inside the motorhome, only closing the screen door.

"What do you think's on his mind?" Dana whispered.

"He'll probably make up some cock and bull story to try to convince Sarah to trust him again."

"I think Sarah's smarter than that."

Seated next to Sarah, Grosler took her hand. "I've missed you. I know you have doubts about me because of my stupid lie, and I want to make it up to you."

Sarah withdrew her hand. "I can't trust anyone who lies to me. You must have realized that someone would catch you in that whooper you've been telling."

His chin briefly touched his chest. "I lost my contract with the travel magazine when it went out of business, and I was running low on money. But I was able to go on a speaking circuit to earn some cash when I said I had freelanced for *National Geographic*."

"Then what are you doing here in the resort?"

"I was working on a project based in Texas, hoping to sell it to an RV magazine."

"So you're traveling around the country in your

motorhome photographing—?"

"Actually I'm a photojournalist. I also write about the places I've been. This was supposed to be a brief stopover, but I heard that the photography club was looking for a speaker. They only paid a small stipend, but it came in handy. Then I met you."

"Are you planning to continue to lie about your work?"

"No, Sarah. I just got a call from another magazine. They want me to do an extensive photo layout. That's why I stopped to say goodbye for now."

Sarah was unsure whether she should believe a man who had blatantly lied to so many people. Maybe he *had* been desperate but that didn't absolve him of deceiving people.

"Will you still be here when I return next month?"

"I'm not sure. Our plans are indefinite."

"I hope so because I enjoy your company."

"Before you go, tell me what happened when you were hit on the head."

He sighed. "The sun was in my eyes when I left my golf cart and I didn't see whoever it was that hit me. The next thing I knew I was in the hospital having my head mummified."

His smile made Sarah's knees tremble. He must be telling the truth or they wouldn't have kept him in the hospital. "Do you have a concussion?"

"Yes, but it's nothing I can't manage."

"Take care," she said, rising from her chair.

"I'll send you postcards from wherever I happen to land."

She smiled and was surprised when he leaned to kiss her goodbye.

"I'll be thinking of you, Sarah." He turned and left.

Dana had been peering through the curtains when

Bob delivered his kiss. Sarah noticed her duck back out of sight and was angry that she had been spied on. She was about to rush back inside when Harry's golf cart pulled onto the lot.

"Howdy, Miss Sarah," he said, dismounting from the cart and sweeping off his Stetson.

Sarah sat down and waited for him. Remembering what Rosie had told her, her anger intensified. It must have shown on her face because Harry's forward motion slowed, the smile on his face dissapating.

"What's wrong, pretty lady?"

"Sit down," she demanded. "We need to talk."

Harry replaced his hat and took a seat on the opposite side of the table instead of his usual chair beside her. His eyebrows raised and he looked at her expectantly.

"I heard today that you're the resort Casanova. That you have lady friends everywhere."

"Who told you that? Rosie?"

"How'd you know?"

"She's jealous 'cause I don't go over there anymore to help her out since her husband died."

"Why not?"

"'Cause I've been spendin' time with you."

Sarah sighed and closed her eyes. "I don't believe in breaking up relationships, Harry."

"No relationship to it, Miss Sarah, except in her mind. I'm free, white and sixty-five, so I can spend time with anybody I durn well choose."

Sarah heard her named called. Dana was standing on the motorhome steps.

"Walter just received a phone call from Sheriff Brandson's office. Paul Gates has been found."

Sarah left the patio. "Where?"

"You're not going to believe this but he's in the hospital. He says he was involved in a car accident."

"This is getting serious, Dana. I think we'd better hire a bodyguard."

"Not a bad idea," Water said, standing inside the screen door. "I'll ask Steve for a recommendation. And it might be a good idea to visit Gates in the hospital."

"Mind if I go along?" Harry said. "Paul and I are friends. If he won't talk to you, he will to me. I'll just go on home and change clothes."

Sarah smiled. Harry did have male friends. Rosie had been lying. "We'd be pleased to have you come along," she said, taking his hand.

Walter scowled but said nothing more. She knew what he was thinking, but he was wrong. Harry was too nice to kill anyone, like his friend Jerome.

Chapter Fifteen

"Sarah, you're becoming quite the social butterfly," Walter said as they were boarding the Jeep. "Two men buzzing around you like honey bees."

"It's about time. I haven't had a male companion since my husband Terry died."

Dana smiled. "Shall we have dinner at the new restaurant in town after we leave the hospital?"

While Walter navigated the narrow streets through the resort, they speculated about their various suspects. With so many RVers in residence, they knew they had only scratched the surface. He reminded them that his flight was scheduled for five the following afternoon, so they would have to scramble to check out any remaining leads. He also warned them again about investigating on their own.

"I'm still wondering who that dark-haired woman and her companion are," Sarah said. "I should have asked Harry about them. By the way, don't forget to pick him up. I hope he's not disappointed about our invitation for a home cooked meal."

Walter laughed. "I think he'll settle for dinner out with you. Even with Dana and I along."

"There he is, standing outside his motorhome waiting for us. Be nice to him, Walt. He'll provide us with valuable information about Varina's blackmail victims."

Grinning, Harry boarded the Jeep and took the remaining seat next to Sarah. Before he had time to say hello, Sarah began interrogating him about the illusive couple in the blue golf cart.

"Sounds like Bill and Cara from Saint Louie."

"Friends of the Zagoris?"

He hesitated. "I wouldn't call 'em friends. They're just neighbors that live a few lots down from Jerome."

"Did they get along with Varina?"

"Not many people did and I don't think Cara was one of 'em."

"Varina must have hit on Cara's husband."

"Most likely," he said, squeezing Sarah's hand.

Sarah wondered why they hadn't seen the blue golf cart when they passed the lot. Harry explained that they kept the cart in a small shed beside their RV. She then told him about the couple spying at the outdoor restaurant.

"I reckon they heard you were investigatin' Varina's death. They musta been curious about what you found out."

"But why would they make a U turn in the middle of the street to get away from us?"

"That's somethin' I'll ask 'em tomorrow."

"Do it casually," Walter said. "You won't want them to think you're investigating them."

Harry laughed. "Oh, I'll be cool." Turning to Sarah, he smiled.

Sarah's heart thumped against her chest. *I think I'm*

in love.

Twenty minutes later they pulled into a parking space at the hospital. When they reached the elevator, Walter instructed Harry to visit his friend alone. When he learned what had happened, he would ask Paul if they could visit him. Harry stepped off the elevator to make his way to the nurse's station while the others found seats in the waiting room. Nearly half an hour later, Harry returned frowning. "The nurse came in to sedate him, so I had to leave before I could ask if he'd talk to you."

"What did he tell you about the accident?" they all asked at once.

Harry looked about the waiting room, which had filled in his absence. "I think we better talk in the Jeep."

Agreeing, they trooped back to the elevator, rode down to the first floor, and exited the building. Once they were seated in the Jeep, Walter said. "Let's hear it."

"Paul said his client didn't show up at the office but he called a few minutes after their appointment time. He asked Paul to meet him at a restaurant out north on the highway. On the way there, Paul's brakes conked out and the car ran off the road on a curve into a grove of trees. He musta been drivin' awful fast."

"The main brake line must have been punctured," Walter said. "Gates must not have seen the dashboard warning light."

Dana reminded Walter that he hadn't noticed the warning light on her Jeep before the accident.

"How badly is the realtor hurt?" Sarah asked.

"His arm's broke and he's got head injuries. He's also got some cracked ribs. His car was stuck between two trees for a coupla days before anybody spotted it. Lucky the car didn't catch fire."

"One less suspect," Turning to Harry, Sarah said, "Be careful. When the killer finds out you're investigating the case, he's liable to damage your car as well."

"Would you come to see me in the hospital, Miss Sarah?"

"Of course I would." *I hope it's not the morgue.*

The alarm sounded at six the next morning. Dana groaned and rolled out of bed to wake Sarah. She could hear Walter moving about in the kitchen and smelled coffee brewing. The man never seemed to sleep. She was going to miss him and had to admit she was worried about their safety once he was gone. She hoped Sarah was right about Harry. He could prove a valuable asset, if the killer didn't put *him* in the hospital.

Why was the killer continuing his reign of terror? He was simply calling attention to himself. Dana had given up on the theory that the murderer was a woman. She doubted that any female would have gone to such lengths to confuse investigators. Crawling beneath two cars to puncture the main brake line was definitely not something most women would do. Especially those over the age of fifty.

Sarah groaned when she touched her shoulder. Mumbling Harry's name, she turned her back on Dana and continued to sleep. Might as well let Sarah enjoy her dream while she talked to Walter in the kitchen, although she still wasn't ready to discuss their future.

He was arranging strips of bacon in a skillet when she opened the pocket door. "I didn't know you could cook," she said, rubbing sleep from her eyes.

He smiled. "Who do you think feeds me when you're not around?"

"No other women in your life to cook for you?"

"Not that I've noticed."

"Before you leave, we need to talk to the office manager and his wife. Remember the *J* on the golf ball? And the card signed 'All my love, Varina" Too bad you weren't able to get more information from Dressler's receptionist."

Walter sighed. "I had hoped we could spend some time alone before I leave."

I just can't do this yet, Walter. "Plenty of time for that once you retire next month."

"So you're not giving up on the case? How can I go back to my job knowing you're still in danger?"

"Harry will gather information while we stay close to home."

"I'm not sure we can trust him."

"Life's a gamble, Walter."

"But you're not willing to gamble on me."

"I have so far, and Wyoming's the place to discuss our future. Not here. Not now."

The pocket door slid open and Sarah's sleepy voice said, "Do I smell something burning?"

Walter turned back to the range, cursing beneath his breath. "Forget the bacon. Looks like we'll have hotcakes for breakfast."

"Speaking of hot, when are you questioning the office manager?"

Dana grimaced. "You think Jeffrey Dressler is hot?"

"Full of fire and brimstone. Today's the last day Walter can talk to him."

"And we can talk to his wife."

Walter put a lid on the smoking skillet and set it in the sink. "Okay, gals, this morning I'll have a talk with Mister Dressler, but what excuse can you use to talk to his wife?"

Sarah smiled. "We'll think of something."

Taking his mug of coffee to the dining nook, he said, "Don't get too gabby. If you're not back here in two hours, I'll come looking for you."

"So you think Dressler's wife knew about his affair with Varina and killed her?"

"Entirely possible. Dana. Be careful."

When Walter left the motorhome at nine that morning, the two women sat in the dining nook discussing their strategy. Sarah had looked up the Dresslers in the directory and they knew the wife's name was Camille. They decided to say they were new to the resort and that Harry had suggested they meet her because they'd enjoy her company. She could tell them about all the resort activities.

"Sounds good to me. We can also express our fears about the murder."

"That should get her to open up about Varina."

Sarah drove the golf cart onto the Dressler lot half an hour later. Parking behind an elaborate red and gold cart with a surrey top, they knocked at the motorhome door.

"Pretty expensive rig for an office manager," Sarah whispered.

"Maybe they won the lottery."

The door opened and a woman as tall as Dana stood on the landing. Dressed in a royal blue workout suit, the middle aged, ash blonde held a coffee mug.

"Hi," Sarah said. "We're new to the resort and—"

"I know who you are." She motioned them inside.

Surprised, they looked at each other and shrugged. Once inside she told them to be seated in a pair of plush leather chairs, then asked the reason for their visit. Sarah said that Harry told them to ask about the activities schedule.

"That's something you should ask about at the office. Who's Harry?"

"Harry Clasbergan. He said you were someone we should get to know."

"Really? I can't imagine why."

Sarah was frustrated by the turn of events and put off by the woman's attitude.

"We're also concerned about the murder," Dana said.

"That's understandable. If I pulled a body from the lake, I'd be concerned too."

She asked if Camille suspected anyone of killing Varina Zagori. Her answer was a resounding no. She had heard they were investigating the woman's death and wondered why they didn't defer to the sheriff.

She was told about the ruined tires, break-ins, and punctured brake line that caused an accident. Dana then touched her temple, which was still discolored. Camille's response was that they should stay in their motorhome and stop playing Jessica Fletcher.

"We have investigated and solved a number of murders," Sarah said. "And this one has gotten personal."

Camille Dressler frowned. "I hope you don't suspect me. I had no reason to kill Varina."

Sarah exchanged glances with Dana. Should they bring up the greeting card? Dana nodded so Sarah told her about the card they had seen in her husband's office signed by Varina Zagori.

Camille jumped to her feet to stand over Sarah, asking what it said. Cowed by the woman, Sarah repeated, "All my love, Varina."

"I don't believe it."

"Then I suggest you go to your husband's office to find the card."

"And I suggest you leave."

Both women got to their feet and made a hasty exit. When Sarah backed the golf cart from the lot, she said, "I guess I shouldn't have told her, Dana."

"I wish we could be there for the confrontation. Walter's there now. I think I'd better warn him." Dana punched in his number on her cell. The phone rang several times before he answered. When she briefly filled him in on the situation, he groaned.

"Thanks for letting me know."

Sarah pulled onto their lot and Dana left the golf cart to unlock the motorhome door. "You should have told him to stand back and watch the explosion. Too bad he's not wearing a flak jacket."

"From her reaction, I don't think Camille Dressler's the killer. She seemed genuinely shocked at the news. But how could she possibly not know? News travels in this place with the speed of a guided missile."

"Maybe because Varina was involved with so many men that nobody seems to care anymore. Her exploits have probably become passé."

"Except for the wives. I wish I hadn't told Camille about her husband. It may cause a divorce, but who needs a cheating husband?"

Dana sat down heavily in her chair, reaching to pet Jenny, who licked her hand. "I don't think Walter's happy with us right now, but maybe the Dresslers will let something slip." She imaged them screaming at each other in Walter's presence.

The motorhome door opened a few minutes later. Walter was grinning when he stepped inside. When they looked up expectantly, he said, "That was some fireworks you two set off."

"What happened, Walter?"

He said that he had arrested angry women, but the Dressler woman topped them all. She entered the office like an angry bull and rummaged through desk drawers as though looking for a winning lottery ticket. When she found the card she attacked her husband with both feet and hands. Walter had pulled her off before her husband was badly injured.

"What did Dressler do after the attack?"

"He asked me to leave."

Sarah smiled "I wish I had been a mosquito on the wall."

Walter lowered himself to the couch. "You two need a bodyguard." He took out his cell phone and called the sheriff's office. When he clicked off, he said, "Your bodyguard will be here sometime today. Sheriff Brandson called the best guard he knows while I was on the phone."

Both women sighed. Dana hoped he would be as effective as Jeff Mailer, their Wyoming bodyguard.

"I'm sure he is, Love. But where will he sleep?"

"We'll have to rent him an RV and park it in the empty lot next door. That's what I should have done for you."

He frowned. "You know I wouldn't have slept there."

Both women thanked him for arranging their protection. Walter's own relief was evident in his eyes. Now he wouldn't have to worry about them until his retirement. He checked his watch. "Six more hours and I'll be leaving on the plane. Anything else you need me to do?"

"Not a thing, Walter. By the way, did Dressler say anything important?"

"Not nearly enough. He was just beginning to open

up when his wife came storming in. I doubt we'll get anything else out of him."

Sarah and Dana groaned. Their timing had been terrible. Dressler was definitely a suspect, although Sarah wondered whether he would have kept Varina's card if he'd murdered her. Then again, he might have killed her in a fit of passion and now regretted his actions.

"What worries me most is that both Dresslers will want to kill the messenger. You two are in more danger than ever. I suggest you keep the door locked and not answer it for anyone."

"What about Harry, Walt?"

"Don't go anywhere with him or Grosler without your bodyguard."

Sarah sighed heavily. Another chaperone? Harry was their lifeline. He couldn't possibly be involved in the murder. He hadn't stopped by and she wondered what had become of him. Had he too been involved in an accident?

A knock sounded moments later and Walter rose to answer. Sarah sighed with relief when she heard Harry's voice. Her cowboy entered the coach with a bouquet of flowers and she stood to give him a hug. They then sat together on the couch while Dana searched for something that would serve as a vase.

Standing over them, Walter said, "I'm trusting you to look after the ladies. A bodyguard's on his way but one man isn't enough. He has to have time to sleep."

Harry shook his head so hard that he resembled a bobble doll. "I'll stand guard whenever I'm needed, sir."

"Good. See that you do. You can work out a schedule with the bodyguard. He's going to be spending his nights in an RV next door."

Sarah said she was glad that Walter had finally

decided that Harry was trustworthy. He had checked out clean and apparently didn't have an uncontrollable temper. He doubted that Harry would get involved with anyone like Varina Zagori.

Harry's grin was so wide that his wisdom teeth were visible. He said he had never been in trouble and that he would take good care of the ladies. He then asked if he could take Miss Sarah for a walk.

"I'm afraid not," Walter said. "There's always the possibility of a deliberate hit and run."

"What about Jenny?" Sarah said. "Somebody has to take *her* for a walk."

The sheriff said they would drop her off at a kennel on the way to the airport. Jenny barked as though she objected. Their wolf dog almost seemed human.

Harry volunteered to walk the dog but was told that his life was also in danger. He was welcome to accompany them to the airport if the bodyguard hadn't arrived, but he needed to keep his own driving to a minimum.

Walter advised them to stock up on groceries on their return trip from the airport. He said that Sheriff Brandson had added two extra men to patrol the resort, so hopefully the killer will be stymied in his attempts to cause more accidents.

"Why'd you 'spose the killer's doin' all this stuff?"

Walter shook his head. "It doesn't make much sense unless he's trying to eliminate more people and can't get it right."

Dana reminded them that Varina Zagori had been killed with precision, a golf ball to the temple and carried to the lake and drowned.

"How'd you know she wasn't hit by a stray ball and fell in the water unconscious, Miss Dana?"

"She would have fallen face forward and floated

into the weeds. We found her face up so someone must have carried her into the weeds and pushed her head beneath the water until she drowned."

They hadn't told him about the orange ball because the only other person who knew about the ball, other than the police, was the killer. They theorized that, whoever the killer was, he would eventually let that slip.

Dana was reminded that she needed to rent an RV. Harry told them about someone in the resort they could talk to. Pulling out his wallet he retrieved a card and handed it to her, saying that Garrett Brown would deliver a fifth wheel trailer that day. Sighing with relief, she called and was told the delivery would occur within the hour.

"You're a real lifesaver, Harry. What would we do without you?"

Walter suggested that the two of them spend some time together on the patio while he had a talk with Dana. They were happy to comply. Once they left the RV and seated themselves at the table, Harry pulled a small box from his pocket and handed it to Sarah. "A friendship ring."

Sarah gasped when she opened the box. It resembled an engagement ring and she was afraid to touch it. Harry took the box from her and placed the ring on her finger, declaring it a perfect fit.

A sleek fifth wheel trailer arrived half an hour later as Sarah and Harry were quietly talking on the patio. Harry left his seat to help direct the trailer toter as he backed the RV onto the lot.

"Nice bachelor pad," he said when the driver left without hooking up the utility hoses. "Is the bodyguard goin' to cook his own meals or take them with you?"

"Good question. I hope he arrives before we leave for the airport." As she spoke, a nondescript beige sedan pulled along the curb. A moment later a tall, gray haired man stepped from the car and waved. Handsome to a fault, he walked over, extending his hand. Harry didn't appear happy to see him.

"Greg Stanton," he said. "Your new bodyguard."

Sarah noticed his wedding ring. He must be married to a gorgeous woman who was going to miss him terribly, unless she came to stay with him in the trailer. But wouldn't that distract him from his job?

Dana and Walter left the motorhome to greet him. When the introductions had been made and a brief summary of their situation, Sarah volunteered to show him his accommodations. Harry wasn't far behind.

Once they checked to make sure the trailer was in good condition, Sarah asked about their bodyguard's wife. "Is she coming here to stay?"

"No, she travels a lot with her job, so we don't see each other that often."

"Do you cook, or will you be eating with us next door?"

He smiled. "I can cook but I won't turn down a dinner invitation."

Sarah told him about their trip to the airport and asked that he trail along behind. Greg agreed and parked his car beside the RV. Harry followed Sarah to the motorhome like a whipped puppy.

"Less than three hours until takeoff," Walter said. "Tell me now if there's anything I need do before I leave."

The letdown Dana experienced when Walter's plane took flight was close to unbearable. How would they manage without him? She glanced at Greg Stanton and smiled halfheartedly. He seemed capable as he continued to scan the airport crowd, but he wasn't Walter. She walked over to inform him about their planned trip to a grocery store, and he seemed relieved that he could stock up on food. He assured her that he wouldn't lose them in traffic.

Sarah sat in the passenger seat, leaving Harry alone in the back, still apparently sulking. Was he actually jealous of their bodyguard? Dana smiled at the thought and decided to question him about the resort residents.

She eyed him briefly in the rearview mirror. "You must have formed an opinion about the killer's identity by now, Harry."

He didn't speak for several moments. "I've got my suspicions, Miss Dana."

"Who stands out in your mind?"

"That California fellah, the one with the gold plated lot numbers, has been on my mind."

"Why?"

"He's rich enough to buy the whole resort and he doesn't take no for an answer."

"So you think that if Varina tried to blackmail him, he decided to erase her from his life?"

"I wouldn't be surprised."

"Anyone else?"

"I wouldn't put it past that photographer. A man with a forked tongue has no morals and would probably not think twice about killin' somebody."

Sarah gasped. "Why do you think Bob killed Varina? He hasn't been here long and he's not married. If he doesn't have a wife, how could Varina blackmail him?"

Harry's voice grew fainter. "Maybe it was about him workin' for *National Geographic*."

"He doesn't have enough money to blackmail," Sarah said, sounding as though she were defending

Grosler.

Dana glanced at Sarah's crimson face and decided to change the subject. "What's for dinner tonight, Sarah? Let's plan something special."

"How about barbequed pig with an apple stuffed in his mouth."

Chapter Sixteen

Dinner in the motorhome was strained. Sarah ignored Harry, focusing her attention instead on Greg Stanton. Dana thought she should be slapped for treating Harry so badly. The meal was saved from abysmal failure when Dana asked about Greg's clients. Told he couldn't discuss them by name or location, he entertained his dinner companions with humorous stories of couples who hired him to protect them from each other.

When Greg asked Harry about his cattle ranch, the cowboy described it as an ordinary herd of long-horned steers. Pretending to yawn, he left shortly after dinner. Shrugging, Sarah filled Greg in all the things that had happened since their arrival. He took notes and remarked that the killer's actions were peculiar.

"Usually, someone who commits a crime tries to make himself invisible. I've rarely heard of a killer who called attention to himself."

"What about Son of Sam and Jack the Ripper?" Sarah said. "I've read about a number of killers who taunted police with notes bragging about their murders."

"That's true, but they were serial killers. There only seems to be one victim in this case."

"The sheriff's investigating *five* murders and doesn't know whether they're related. And don't forget the two brake line punctures," Dana reminded him.

"Failed brakes are not always a death sentence. There are easier ways to kill someone. The punctures seem more like a warning than an attempt to kill."

Sarah leaned toward him. "There's also the small gray vest with a large phoenix button. What do you make of that?"

Greg said, "There's obviously some hidden meaning. Or simply an attempt to confuse the issue. Have you tried researching phoenix rising?"

Dana said she had conducted some research on the Internet and found an organization by that name, which linked a poor diet with chronic fatigue syndrome. There were also television programs, musical groups and songs, and a novel by that name. "For the life of me, I can't connect any of those things with the murder."

"The vest looks like part of an old army uniform I saw in a museum," Sarah said. "It was the same color and had a similar button."

"It's probably just another clue to confuse the investigators. It seems the killer is playing games."

"That's what Walter said and I've come to the same conclusion. Nothing else makes sense."

Greg asked about the photographer who left the resort. "I thought everyone was on lockdown."

Sarah smiled. "He's just a renter who hasn't been here long, and must have gotten permission to leave because of his job assignment."

"So you don't think he's involved in any way?"

"Not at all."

Dana drummed her fingers on the table. "I wouldn't

be too sure. He's been lying about working for *National Geographic* to get on a speaking circuit."

Greg's brows lifted. He asked if Grosler had known the murder victim.

"He said he didn't, but I can't believe anyone who lies to me."

"He needed the money," Sarah protested. "The magazine he worked for went out of business."

Greg advised Sarah to steer clear of Bob until the killer was apprehended.

Sarah sighed. "He won't be back until next month, so it's a moot point."

Their bodyguard handed them both a card with his cell number, telling them to call if they heard anything unusual during the night. Now that Jenny was in the kennel, they no longer had an early warning system. He suggested installing a bell or buzzer on the door to wake them at night.

Sarah said that she would rather have Jenny there, but Greg warned that the dog could be poisoned. When he left for the night, Dana scolded her friend for the way she'd treated Harry. "The poor man will probably never come back."

"I don't care. He's jealous of Greg and was running Bob down. And he's the resort Casanova."

"I thought Rosie spread that rumor to get Harry back. I think you're making a mistake, Sarah. He seems genuinely interested in you and I doubt he's a womanizer."

"I think you're making an even bigger mistake. Holding Walt at arm's length will push him into the arms of another woman."

Dana was shocked by Sarah's attitude. During the four years they'd been friends, they'd never had a serious disagreement. She watched as Sarah trooped off to bed without another word. Leaning back in her recliner, she closed her eyes to think. Was Sarah right? Was she on the verge of losing Walter? She couldn't imagine life without him. Maybe she should give him a call. Her cell rang before she could leave her chair. The caller I.D. said it was him.

"Dana, my plane just got in—"

"I was about to call. Where are you?"

"Standing in the window of my apartment looking at the city lights Why were you planning to call? Did something happen?"

"No, I just wanted to say I love you."

She heard a pop in the background and silence until Walter gasped. "I've been shot." Shocked, she heard him fall and repeatedly called his name. Frantic, she screamed for Sarah, telling her to bring her cell phone. When Sarah arrived, she handed her the phone, telling her to listen for Walter's voice. Then, using Sarah's phone, she called 911. Telling the operator what had happened, she gave her the area code and pleaded that she immediately call for an ambulance.

Sarah reported no sound on Walter's end of the line, so Dana called Greg. He was there in less than a minute. She briefly told Sarah what had happened before Greg arrived. Sarah hugged her and sat down beside her to pray.

Greg said, "Please calm down, Miz Logan. If Sheriff Grayson was able to tell you he was shot, the wound must not be fatal. I'll call the sheriff's office here and ask them to find out about his condition."

Dana thanked him and wondered aloud if the killer had followed Walter to California.

"He told me he was working on two murder cases when he left, one of them a suspected psycho killer. That's probably who's responsible."

"But Walter just got home. How would anyone know?"

Greg said someone could have been waiting outside his apartment and noticed his lighted window. Perhaps a criminal recently released from prison who wanted revenge."

Dana's hand flew to her chest. "I never realized how dangerous his job is." Hot tears scorched her face although her body felt numb.

"He'll be all right, Dana. I feel it in my heart." Sarah handed back the phone and Dana listened for a sound that would tell her he was still alive. "If he pulls through, we need to go to him."

"We need permission to fly there." She accepted Sarah's offer of a soothing cup of chamomile tea, knowing it would be a long night.

When Greg ended his call, he said Sheriff Brandson probably wouldn't allow the trip to California until his department thoroughly checked out the shooting incident. "That could be tomorrow or as long as a couple of days."

Dana thought she heard the faint sound of a siren on Walter's phone, but it was probably wishful thinking. Holding her hand for silence, she pressed the phone so close to her ear that it hurt. Long moments passed before she heard the sound of a door hitting the wall and men's excited voices. She then remembered to place the call on speaker phone.

Dana repeatedly yelled hello into the phone but no one answered. She then heard someone say, "He's still alive. Start an IV and get him on the gurney."

"Thank God." What would have happened if they hadn't been talking on the phone when he was shot? Tears streaming down her face, Dana refused to consider his death. Sarah grasped her hand and they prayed again for his survival.

Chapter Seventeen

Next morning, after little sleep, Dana received a call from the sheriff's office. Walter was still alive although in serious condition. She was given the name and number of the hospital and told that she and Sarah had permission to fly to California. She immediately phoned the hospital and was told that Walter was unable to take calls.

Reservations needed to be made. Calling as soon as she looked up the airline's number, she learned there was a flight available at midnight, with a layover in Denver. Dana made reservations for the three of them before calling Greg. Apologizing for rousing him early, she said they had a few things to investigate before they left.

"Do you think that's wise?"

"Maybe not but I can't sit here in the motorhome all day worrying about Walter."

"I'll be over as soon as I pack. Don't leave your RV until I get there."

Sarah stood yawning in her robe, asking about the

call. When Dana filled her in, she said she needed to talk to Harry before they left. "I'd never forgive myself if something happens to him while we're gone."

"Maybe you should call him, although he might not want to talk to you."

"We didn't exchange phone numbers," Sarah opened a cupboard to retrieve a frying pan. "If he doesn't show up, I'll know he's through with me."

"I don't think Harry will give up that easily. He'll probably want to make the trip with us, but I doubt the sheriff will allow him to leave."

"Why? He's not a witness."

"Living across the street from Jerome Zagori might make him a witness for the prosecution, *if* the murder case ever goes to trial."

"They can't keep suspects locked in here forever."

"Just until the investigation's over."

Someone knocked at the door and Sarah rushed to the bedroom to dress. She obviously didn't want anyone to catch her in her robe sans makeup and uncombed hair.

A sad faced Harry stood at the door asking for Miss Sarah. Dana invited him in. When she told him about Walter, she thought he was going to cry. Such a nice, sweet man. How could Sarah treat him so badly? He offered to look after the motorhome while they were gone, which surprised Dana. Did he have an ulterior motive? No, it was just paranoia creeping in again.

The pocket door slid open and Sarah's face lit up when she noticed Harry. Sitting beside him on the couch, she took his hand.

"I know about Sheriff Walt." His expression was even gloomier. "I came over early to tell you somethin' I should have said before, but I was worried about your reaction."

"About what, Harry?"

"I know you like Bob Grosler but I think you should know he's Rosie's son."

Sarah gasped. "How do you know?"

"I saw a framed picture of him in Rosie's coach. When she saw me lookin,' she put the it in a drawer."

Dana stopped making coffee to ask, "Did she admit that he's her son?"

"No, but he resembles Rosie's husband, who died not long ago."

"Then I think we'd better talk to Rosie before we leave."

Harry said if she wouldn't admit her motherhood to *him*, she certainly wouldn't tell the two of them. They had become friends since her husband's death and she didn't seem to get along well with other residents. "She's been awful cranky since Alan died."

Sarah wondered why Bob didn't mention his mother. They decided to pay Rosie a visit that morning. Maybe she and Bob were estranged, which could explain their reluctance to admit their relationship. Harry left shortly thereafter, promising to return that afternoon. Sarah had refused his dinner invitation, telling him Walter had advised them not to dine in public. Dana would have asked him to dinner but didn't want to risk a repeat of the previous night.

After breakfast, they left in Greg's sedan for Dana's new lot. Rosie was already at work in her flower garden when they arrived and didn't seem to welcome company. Sarah openly admired Rosie's flowers and asked if they could have cuttings for Dana's flower garden. That seemed to soften her up enough to talk.

"I'll bet you miss your son Bob, now that he's gone," Sarah said.

Rosie tossed her trowel onto the pavement. "I don't

have a son. Never wanted kids. They're a pain in the patootie. I'm happy with my two Siamese cats. They keep me plenty of company and they don't talk back!"

Sarah glanced at Dana. "Sorry, I could have sworn you had a son named Bob."

"Don't know where you heard that, unless it came from Harry. That old fool gets everything mixed up."

Sarah thanked her for the offer of cuttings and they left for Dana's lot. Briefly inspecting the planting area, they left.

"Where to now?" Greg asked.

"Back to the motorhome to pack for the trip. Then we'll look up Rosie and Bob on the people locator."

"Sounds like a plan," their bodyguard said as he navigated the resort's narrow streets. "Have you two ever considered opening a detective agency?"

Sarah laughed. "I thought about it and dismissed it in the same breath."

Dana called the hospital again when they reached the motorhome. Walter was still listed in serious condition and not taking calls. Frustrated, she packed, mindlessly tossing clothing into a suitcase. She then booted up her laptop computer. She found Rosie Darcun's name and clicked on criminal records. "Look at this," she said when Greg leaned over her shoulder to read what she'd found.

"Rosie was arrested for assaulting a neighbor in Pittsburg. Charges were dropped when a financial settlement was paid to the neighbor."

"Was the neighbor attacked with a weapon?"

"Doesn't say. Maybe she just slapped her."

"When did it happen?"

Dana scrolled down the page. "Looks like nineteen-eighty seven. She was much younger then."

"What about relatives?"

"There are two men's names listed: Alan and Marcus Darcun. It doesn't say how they're related but Harry called Rosie's husband Alan."

"Maybe you'll find the old woman listed under Marcus Darcun's name."

Dana typed in his name and found little information about him. "His age is fifty-eight, but no relatives' names are listed. It says he's from upstate New York. That's strange. He has more of an upper Midwestern accent, like Wisconsin, Minnesota or the Dakotas."

"He could have been born there and moved with his family further west."

Dana sighed. It was difficult to keep her mind off Walter, but she knew she had to stay busy so that she wouldn't cry herself sick. Who else could she investigate online? She typed in Jeffrey Dressler's name. He had no criminal record, but that didn't mean he was innocent. The card from Varina qualified him as a suspect.

That left Paul and Lacey Gates. She typed in Paul's name and found Lacey listed as well as three other names: Susan, Carol and Michael, which she assumed were their children. Paul and Lacey also had no criminal records, and she wondered how Paul was faring after his accident. Picking up her cell phone, she called the hospital. A receptionist said he would be released that afternoon. Perhaps they should take him flowers and ask about the accident before their trip to California.

The golden state reminded her of the Rosenbines in lot 800. Stan's name came up and she found Alberta's name as well as Stanley Junior. The men were clean but Alberta had been arrested for taking part in a protest demonstration during the late

1990s. Dana sighed. With the exception of Rosie, her research had been a waste of time. Despite a lack of criminal records, any one of the suspects could have committed the murder.

Sarah prepared lunch while Dana continued her research. Their afternoon dragged on until Harry showed up with more flowers. Where was he getting them? The flowers reminded her of the bouquet they planned to take to Paul Gates. Harry's flowers would wilt while they were gone, so maybe he wouldn't mind a requisition.

When Sarah led Harry out to the patio, Dana decided to pick Greg's brain. She said, "From what we've told you about the suspects, which one seems the most likely to have committed the murder?"

Greg thought for a moment. "Let's go over them one at a time."

"First, the wealthy Californian who told Varina he would leave his wife and meet her in Hawaii. He had the most to lose."

"But would he have killed her himself or hired someone to do it for him?"

"Probably hired a hit man who played golf."

"Why? You said the golf ball had been hit close to the woman's head. That doesn't take much skill. You also said the ball was an inexpensive one. Would a rich man buy cheap balls?"

Dana chewed her lip. "Probably not, but if he hired someone—"

"Would a hit man be careless enough to use a ball with his initial on it?"

Dana shook her head. "What about Stan's wife Alberta?"

"If she's away most of the time, she probably doesn't care that her husband had a mistress. They might even have an open marriage."

"True." Dana ran over the other suspects in her mind. Paul and Lacey Gates, Jerome Zagori, Bob Grosler, Jeffrey and Camille Dressler, the McKinseys, Rosie Darcun. Harry? No, she had dismissed Harry as a suspect days earlier. And she still could not imagine tiny Rosie Darcun killing anyone, despite her crankiness and police record.

"Jeffrey Dressler is my prime suspect, or his wife Camille," Dana said. "That card in his office from Varina proves his affair with her."

"Are you sure? Maybe he found the card."

"I'm sure. You should have seen the way he grabbed it from the desk as though the card were a prized possession."

"You said his wife attacked him after you told her about the card?"

"Yes, and she's my height and at least twenty pounds heavier. I think she's quite capable of picking up Varina and carrying her to the lake."

"Is she a golfer?"

"I believe she is. There were two sets of clubs in her golf cart."

"Where could she have hidden the body until she could dispose of it, without her husband knowing?"

Dana thought back to their visit. "If I remember correctly, there's a tarped section under the overhang of their fifth wheel trailer that's used for storage. She could have hidden the body there."

"And where do you think she killed the victim?"

"There's a walled-in section around the patio that's about four feet high. She could have invited Varina over and drugged her drink, then laid her on the ground and driven the ball into her temple."

He smiled. "Sounds feasible, especially if the murder

was premeditated."

Dana was elated. Had they solved the murder? Camille Dressler not only had the opportunity and motive, she also had the means. But what about the initial *J* on the ball? Was she trying to frame her husband Jeffrey for the murder? She wouldn't be the first to frame a spouse. Countless betrayed people had paved the way for her.

"What about the other suspects?" he asked.

"Paul Gates is leaving the hospital this afternoon."

"Could he have staged the accident?"

"And broken his own arm and ribs?"

Greg sighed. "I guess that is a bit farfetched."

"What if his wife is responsible for his accident for the same reason as Camille Dressler."

"Was she a mechanic in a former life?"

"I guess I need to check that out."

Greg asked about the photographer. "Have you eliminated him as a suspect?"

"Not entirely. There's something strange about that man but Sarah thinks he only lied because he was broke and out of work."

"From what you've said, he not only lied, he was brazen about it. He must have known that someone would trip him up."

Dana remembered reading about the narcissistic syndrome—people who constantly lie and think they're better than everyone else. That seemed to fit Bob Grosler, but she didn't think it included murder.

"It's best to write down all your suspicions and give them to the sheriff. Let him investigate."

Dana reluctantly agreed. "I need to concentrate on Walter from now on."

<><><>

Sarah sat across from Harry at the patio table instead of next to him. She was still upset about his opinions of Bob Grosler, convinced he was attempting to eliminate his competition.

He attempted a lopsided grin but failed miserably. "I'd like to go with you to California to see Walt. I consider him a friend."

"I don't think Sheriff Brandson will allow it, but you can try."

Harry asked for the name and phone number of the hospital where Walter had been transferred. Sarah told him to wait while she got the information from Dana. Moments later she returned smiling.

"Dana thinks she and Greg have solved the murder."

Harry perked up. "Who done it?"

Sarah lowered her voice. "Please promise not to tell anyone."

He crossed his heart.

"Camille Dressler."

"No." Harry shook his head. "She wouldn't kill a flea. She's on the emergency response team that rushes to help people before the ambulance gets here."

Sarah remembered the golf cart that had raced up when Varina's body had been found. That woman must have been Camille.

"She retired from nursin'."

"I've heard of doctors killing their wives and nurses who kill patients in the hospital. I don't think Camille is immune to doing the same thing."

"I don't think she knew about her husband and Varina, so she didn't have a reason to kill her."

"I'll tell them, Harry, but it's going to ruin Dana's day. That and Walter's condition." She said she had to finish packing and suggested he call the sheriff as well as the airlines for a reservation. But she knew that Sheriff Brandson would turn him down.

Chapter Eighteen

The airport was surprisingly crowded. They arrived early for their midnight flight and decided to shop for something to cheer up Walter. Dana picked up three paperback novels by his favorite author, wondering whether he had read them. Placing them back, she reasoned that he wouldn't feel much like reading. She had already ordered three dozen red roses to be sent to his hospital room.

The flowers reminded her of Harry's bouquet, which they had delivered to Paul Gates on his return from the hospital. The visit had been brief with Paul insisting his Honda had been tampered with. He groaned and held his ribs with his uninjured arm whenever he made the slightest movement.

Dana found it difficult to believe that he would deliberately wreck his own car to divert suspicion from himself. Maybe his jealous wife had tampered with the brakes after *she* had killed Varina. Dana remembered Lacey sitting quietly in a corner chair, saying little during their visit. Paul's affair might have infuriated her enough to commit a double murder.

Dana was paying for several magazines when a loud speaker called Sarah's name. Her friend picked up an airport phone and listened. The phone conversation was short and Dana wasn't surprised that the call had come from Harry.

"He tried his best but couldn't get permission to come with us," Sarah said.

"It's probably best that Walter doesn't have many visitors. And we know that Harry will look after things while we're gone."

"If he's not killed before we get back."

"He'll be fine." Dana doubted her own words but didn't want Sarah worrying about him. They had enough problems with Walter. Her last call to the hospital was reassuring. When she told someone at the nurses' station that she was his fiancé, a nurse said he was improving but not yet up to a phone call. Dana left a message that they would be arriving early the following morning.

When they boarded the plane, Sarah managed to fall asleep a few minutes into the flight, but Dana had too much on her mind. From her peripheral vision she noticed their ever vigilant bodyguard surveying the other passengers from across the aisle. She knew he wouldn't sleep until they arrived in Denver for a two hour layover. She doubted he would sleep then.

Dana was sure Sheriff Brandson had only approved their trip because Greg was accompanying them. Sighing with relief, she leaned back against her seat to meditate. Silently reciting her mantra, she drifted into a troubled sleep. Ducks and Canadian geese were pecking at bodies floating in a lake. She must have screamed in her sleep because Greg reached across the aisle to grasp her arm.

"You all right, Miz Logan?"

"You can call me Dana," she said sleepily. "It was just a bad dream." A nightmare actually, but no worse than her life had become since arriving at the resort. She vowed not to take another RV vacation without Walter, if he survived. And no more murder investigations. Dozing off again, she awoke when the pilot announced their approach into Denver.

Sarah had to be shaken awake. She slept like a hibernating bear. When they stumbled down the ramp into the airport, she realized that her fellow passengers were in no better shape than she was. *Add red eye flights to my 'not again' list.*

Greg suggested an early breakfast and they trooped off in search of an all-night restaurant. During the meal he said they should check into the airport hotel for a few hours' sleep before visiting Walter in the hospital. Both women agreed. They didn't want Walter to see them at their worst.

Walter's door was closed when they reached his room. Dana felt her heart catch in her throat when she knocked. A nurse opened the door little more than a crack, telling them to take seats in the waiting room. Walter's bandages were in the process of being changed.

Bandages? How many times had he been shot? Dana felt faint and Greg helped her to the nearest chair. When would this nightmare end?

The nurse came to get them some twenty minutes later, cautioning them to cut their visit short so as not to tire the patient. He was still in serious condition. Walter seemed asleep when they entered his room but opened his eyes when Dana took his hand. Sarah and

Greg stood back to give them privacy.

"Hey, big guy." Dana said as she leaned to lightly kiss his lips.

"Dana, am I dreaming or are you really here?" His voice sounded as though he were in an underground tunnel. Damp strands of gray-streaked hair clung to his brow and he appeared exhausted.

"We came as soon as we could book a flight. How are you feeling?"

"Like someone hammered my chest. Another half an inch and the bullet would have pierced my heart."

Dana's knees trembled and she was grateful when Greg pushed a chair to the bed.

"Marry me, Dana," Walter said. "Here in the hospital so I can die happy."

"You're not going to die. You're too brave and—"

"In love. Please make this old sheriff happy."

"As soon as we can find a minister. A best man and matron of honor are standing by."

Walter smiled and closed his eyes for so long that Dana was tempted to take his pulse. The nurse bustled in, telling them to leave until that afternoon. She seemed disappointed when Dana asked about a clergyman to perform a bedside wedding. Sarah was right about another woman latching onto Walter. It seemed the slim, mature nurse was attracted to him and she wasn't wearing a wedding ring.

When they left his room, Dana decided to talk to Walter's doctor. As his wife, the hospital couldn't deny her information about his condition.

"That's not why you're marrying him, is it, Dana?"

"Of course not. If I had accepted his proposal when he first asked, he wouldn't be lying in the hospital."

"But that's not a good enough reason to get married."

"I love him enough to be his wife, Sarah. I should

have realized it sooner."

"He's a serious hunk, my friend. If you don't marry him, someone else will. That nurse is already trying to get her talons in him."

Dana wasn't worried about losing him to another woman but she was concerned that the sniper would again try to kill him. She asked Greg if he would stand guard to make sure no unsavory characters entered Walter's room. Her bodyguard replied that he had noticed a couple of plain clothes detectives loitering on the third floor. Wondering whether they were there to protect Walter, she was reassured when he said he was certain they were.

"My job," he said, "is to protect the two of you. We can't be sure that the Texas killer hasn't followed us here."

"You don't think that Varina's killer is the one who shot Walter, do you?"

"I doubt it. When Walter left, there was no reason to kill him."

"I need a dress to wear to my wedding," Dana said, distracted. "I didn't pack anything but T-shirts and jeans. We need to go shopping." She glanced at their bodyguard who shrugged.

Sarah decided to buy a new outfit as well. "But first we need to talk to Walter's doctor."

They approached the nurses' station and asked for Doctor Seegraves. Dana had noticed his name listed on the chart above the bed. "If we can't find him in the hospital, we'll look him up in the directory. I have to know Walter's condition."

"They won't tell you until you're married, Dana."

"That won't stop me from trying. I'll get married in my jeans, if necessary. Walter won't mind."

"Of that I'm sure, but I think you need to ask the

doctor what Walter's chances of survival are. *Before* the ceremony."

"If he only has a few hours to live, I'll marry him anyway. I should have accepted his proposal months ago."

Sarah sighed. "I hope you're not doing this out of guilt or pity."

A tear raced down Dana's cheek. "I love the man. I don't know what I'll do if he dies."

Dana finally located Doctor Seegraves at his office. His nurse said he was with a patient and would return her call that afternoon. Dana informed her that Seegraves' patient was getting married in a few hours and that she would appreciate a call before the ceremony. The nurse gasped and promised to deliver the message.

"That should get her off her duff," Sarah said. "Let's go shopping."

"I wish I could call Walter to see how he's doing."

"You know that nurse won't put the call through. She's probably busy trying to seduce him at this very moment. But don't worry. I'm convinced he only has eyes for you or he wouldn't have waited this long."

Dana managed a small laugh. "What would I do without you, Sarah?"

"Oh, you'd do just fine. Once you're married, you won't even know I'm around." Sarah turned to wink at Greg, who lowered his eyes and grinned. "Let's go shopping. No matter what you wear, Walter will think you're the most gorgeous bride in the universe. You know it'll make him happy and help him recover."

They took the elevator down to the main floor and

left the hospital. Asking Greg to drive downtown, they perused a newspaper their bodyguard had acquired that morning. An ad for wedding dresses was featured in the center section. Dana gave Greg the address and he pulled over to punch it into the GPS system. Less than twenty minutes later, they parked in front of the bridal shop.

"A simple dress will do," Dana said as she exited the rental car. Their bodyguard elected to stay in the car two parking spaces back from the main entrance, where he could watch foot traffic. Surprised when they returned in less than an hour, he reported that few people had entered the shop, none of them considered suspicious. It was time to find a minister, whom they knew they should have located sooner. Dana decided to call the bridal shop and was given the name of an ordained minister who specialized in weddings. When she called, he agreed to meet them at the hospital in two hours.

Greg drove them back to the hotel to dress for the ceremony while he waited outside their door. The two women dressed, applied makeup and arranged each other's hair.

"Excited, Dana?"

"Very. This is my third and final wedding and I pray I won't have to bury another husband."

Sarah lifted a water glass, saying, "Here's to Walter's speedy recovery and a long, happy marriage."

A knock sounded and Sarah rushed to the hotel door. Greg stood there frowning. "Phone call from the hospital. The sheriff was taken back into surgery."

"I hope it wasn't the excitement of the wedding," Sarah said "I was afraid Walter was rushing the ceremony."

Noon traffic was heavy and the usual ten minute drive took them nearly half an hour to reach the hospital. Walter was in recovery and they weren't allowed to see him. Dana sat twisting a lace handkerchief, wondering whether the wedding would take place. Berating herself for talking Walter out of early retirement, she knew it was because she was afraid to commit.

Biting her lip until it bled, she noticed mascara-tinged tears staining her short, beige lace wedding dress. Why had she been so stubborn about marrying him? She might have prevented the shooting and maybe even his death. Wiping her face with the handkerchief, she silently begged God to allow Walter to live. She promised to sell the mansion and donate her fortune to charity, if he survived.

A white coated man touched her shoulder. "Missus Grayson? Your husband is asking for you."

Walter was alive and had the presence of mind to ask for his wife. He might have dreamed they were already married while under anesthesia. Dana followed the surgeon into the recovery room where she found Walter awake and groaning. A large bandage covered his chest beneath the flimsy gown, and he feebly extended his hand to her.

"You look like an angel, Love. I'm ready for the ceremony."

"I don't think so, Walter. The strain might be too much for your heart."

He managed a smile. "This old ticker survived a gunshot wound and two surgeries, the last one minor. I'm sure it'll survive a wedding."

Chapter Nineteen

The nurse was waiting when an attendant wheeled Walter into his room. Nurse Crabtree ordered Dana and the wedding party out to the waiting room, but found herself the victim of Walter's ire.

"I'm an officer of the law who's about to get married. I suggest that *you* wait in the hall until after the ceremony."

The nurse turned on her heel and left, glaring at Dana as she walked by. Walter would live. Dana was certain of it. All they needed was the minister, who arrived moments later. Sarah carefully pulled a veil from a large plastic bag and pinned it to the bride's shoulder length auburn hair. She and Greg then moved to the window side of the groom's bed to serve as witnesses.

During the ceremony Walter groaned and placed a hand on his chest. When the minister hesitated, the sheriff insisted he continue. The ceremony was brief, ending with a long kiss. Smiling, Walter said he was the happiest man on the planet. But the revelry was cut short when Doctor Seegraves entered the room and ordered everyone out.

You're too late, Doctor. Dana extended her hand. "I'm Walter's wife. I believe I have a right to be here."

Frowning, he told Sarah and Greg to leave. He then checked Walter's heart. "This nonsense should have waited until after I released you, Sheriff Grayson."

"Best medicine in the world, Doc. I'm so happy, I can't help but get better."

Seegraves took Dana's arm and led her into the hall. "Your husband isn't a young man. See that he doesn't get overly excited."

When Dana insisted he tell her everything about Walter's condition, he said he had an 80% chance of survival, if he followed orders. "He can leave the hospital next week if he progresses well. But no intimacy until after his six week's checkup."

Dana smiled. "No problem, doctor. I'll be leaving for Texas in three days."

"Honeymooning alone?"

"Murder investigation." She didn't elaborate.

Returning to Walter's room, she found him sleeping with the hint of a smile on his face. She retrieved a notepad from her purse and scrawled *I love you and will see you again soon.* Placing the note in his outstretched hand, she lightly kissed his brow and hesitantly left the room.

Sarah and Greg were waiting for her, suggesting a wedding reception lunch in the hospital cafeteria, in case Walter had a setback. During their meal, Dana's cell phone rang, the caller I.D. telling her it was Sheriff Brandson. He first asked about Walter, then gave Dana the bad news. Her motorhome had been spray painted with black letters spelling the word *Killers* on both sides.

"Why is this happening, Sheriff? All we did was find

the body."

"I can't answer that, Miz Logan, but we're getting close to making an arrest."

"That's Missus Grayson, Sheriff. Walter and I were just married."

"But I thought he just had surgery."

"He did but he's a stubborn man."

The sheriff offered his congratulations and said he needed to see both her and Sarah in his office later that week. When she asked why, he said there was a new development that needed addressing. One of his deputies would meet them at the Dallas airport.

Dana relived the past few days during their flight back to Dallas. She'd spent most of her time with Walter while Sarah and Greg played tourists in the state capitol. Her new husband was recuperating well but she hated to leave him in the hospital. She prayed that Sheriff Brandson's investigators had arrested Varina's killer, and that her motorhome could be repainted before they left for home. Why would someone paint graffiti on the RV, unless it was children bent on vandalism? It had to have been painted at night. Nothing about the murder case made sense.

What new development required their consultation? Was Harry or Bob involved? Or Camille Dressler, Lacey Gates, or the Rosenbines, for that matter? Maybe Sheriff Brandson wanted to go over the way the body had been found although the investigator had been thorough when he questioned them. They would know soon enough thanks to their nonstop flight from Sacramento to Dallas.

Dana checked her watch. They should land within

the hour. Closing her eyes, she realized how exhausted she was. She couldn't wait to return home to Wyoming and begin a new life with Walter. A real honeymoon was out of the question until the killer was arrested and her husband had fully recovered.

Sarah awoke from her nap hungry. Dana handed her a bag of peanuts doled out earlier by one of the flight attendants.

"I've been thinking about something Harry told us," Sarah said. "Did you notice how strangely Rosie acted when I asked if Bob was her son?"

"I thought that if he *were* her son, she had disowned him for telling the lie about working for the magazine."

"If he were *my* son, I'd wail the daylights out of him, but I wouldn't disown him."

"I still wonder who hit him on the head."

"He seemed to have recovered before he left the resort."

"We need to concentrate on the other suspects, Sarah. And I'm anxious to talk to Sheriff Brandson."

Sarah said that Lucy Gates and Camille Dressler were her prime suspects. Lucy had been as sullen as a Siamese cat when they took flowers to her husband. "I expected her to be smiling and happy to have him home from the hospital."

Dana shrugged. "She's probably still upset about his affair with Varina."

"I can also imagine Camille carrying Varina to the lake or placing her in a golf cart to drive her there. She's the only woman on our suspect's list capable of getting rid of the body on her own."

"Varina wasn't dead when placed in the lake. The killer took the chance of her coming to and screaming before she drowned."

"I hadn't thought of that, Dana. Maybe the killer

taped Varina's mouth shut before she was carried to the lake."

"I don't think she was in any shape to fight back at that point." From the corner of her eye, Dana noticed Greg place an index finger to his lips, and realized they shouldn't talk about the murder investigation while in flight. The killer might be onboard

A deputy drove them from the airport to the sheriff's office where he turned them over to an investigator. Greg followed in his car and remained outside the room when Dana and Sarah were interrogated, this time on video tape. They agreed later that the interview had made them feel like criminals.

Sarah repeated how she found the victim's body. Dana then reported how the discovery had happened from her vantage point, including how Varina Zagori had been dressed, or undressed, according to one's perspective. They were then shown to an anteroom to wait with Greg for Sheriff Brandson.

"It's all routine," their bodyguard said. "Nothing to worry about if you didn't change your accounts of how you found the body."

Sarah frowned. "So they're just verifying our stories."

Dana asked how he knew the procedure and was told that he was a twenty-five year veteran of the department before recently retiring. No wonder the sheriff had recommended him.

"If the sheriff's ready to make an arrest, why does he need us?" Sarah asked.

"He's checking the facts to make sure his department doesn't make a mistake. Jailing the wrong suspect can lead to a lawsuit."

The door opened and a deputy beckoned them to follow. Greg smiled and gave them a thumb's up as the women left the room. They found Sheriff Brandson with elbows on his desk, his shoulders slumped forward. He appeared as tired as Dana. He half rose from his chair when they entered his office, offering his hand. "Ladies, I appreciate your stopping by. I have a few questions to ask about the Zagori case."

Dana bit her lip to prevent herself from saying the obvious. They weren't there by choice. After the sheriff asked about Walter's condition, he wondered why they thought the killer was tormenting them with vandalism. Had they antagonized anyone when they arrived at the resort?

They both denied contact with anyone before they discovered the body, other than the receptionist at the admittance office. They hadn't had much contact with anyone at first. And no one had threatened them upon arrival.

"Then why do you think you've been harassed?"

Dana hesitated. "My husband thinks the killer has been warning us to stop investigating on our own."

"He's right. You could have gotten yourselves killed. I know about the brake lines and accidents. Both vehicles have been checked for prints and other identifying marks."

"And?" Sarah leaned forward in her chair.

"We're still in the process of acquiring suspect fingerprints."

Disappointed, both women sank deeper in their chairs. Sarah then asked whether they were there for fingerprinting.

He nodded. "We can check yours against a partial palm print found on your motorhome. We dusted the RV after one of your neighbors reported the graffiti."

The sheriff buzzed someone on the intercom and they were led off to be fingerprinted.

Later, after they had been delivered back to the airport parking lot, Greg drove them to the resort, wondering why they hadn't been allowed to drive from the airport to the sheriff's office on their own.

"Procedure," their bodyguard said, and left it at that.

Neither one of them was anxious to view the vandalism, and wished they'd stopped on the way to bring Jenny home from the kennel. She'd been there long enough to forget them.

Once back at the resort, the late afternoon sun illuminated large black letters scrawled across the entire length of the motorhome. In small red letters, the word *beware* was etched at the bottom of the door.

"Looks like nail polish, Dana. It must have been done by a woman."

"Not necessarily. A man could have borrowed it from his significant other."

Dana's cell rang and she noticed the Sacramento area code. Catching her breath, she prayed it wasn't bad news about Walter. She sighed with relief when she heard his voice. After he said he loved her, he reported that he'd fired his nurse.

"Fired her, Walter?"

"Got her transferred to another ward. My new nurse allows me to use the phone."

When he asked about any new developments in the murder case, she thought better of telling him about the graffiti. She did tell him about their visit to the sheriff's office, and that no one had yet been arrested. A woman's voice in the background warned him about excessive conversation, so they exchanged brief goodbyes.

Tired and frustrated, Dana joined her companions

in the motorhome kitchen. A cup of tea was placed before her as she collapsed into the dining nook. It wasn't long before someone knocked at their door. To no one's surprise it was Harry, who wore a troubled expression.

"Sorry about the paint. I tried to scrub it off but it was already dry when I saw it yesterday mornin'."

Dana said not to worry about it. She planned to trade the vandalized RV in on a new one.

Harry's eyes grew larger. "You must have a great deductible."

"As a matter of fact, I'm insurance poor." She shot a warning glance at Sarah, telling her not to contradict her.

"I've been snoopin' around since you left," he said. "I came up with some confusin' stuff you might want to hear."

"Tell us," Sarah said. "What have you learned?"

"Jeff Dressler and Paul Gates' wives moved into a rental trailer."

"Left their husbands?"

"Yeah. They can't move outa the resort yet."

"Gates just got out of the hospital."

"That's what's confusin'. Nobody's there to take care of him."

"Lacey must be mad enough to kill him over his affair."

Dana flinched at Sarah's conclusion. Did the two of them conspire to kill Varina and blame it on their husbands?

Sarah asked if Harry had other news. He hesitated before telling them that Rosie's husband had committed suicide. Dana asked why he hadn't told them sooner.

"She told me not to tell. Ever'body thinks he died of a heart attack. But he shot his self in a field a few miles from here and died in the hospital."

"Did he leave a note?"

"Yeah, but Rosie won't let me read it."

Sarah frowned. "He might have blamed *her*."

"As ornery as she is, I wouldn't doubt it."

Sarah scooted closer "Anything else?"

"'Fraid not but I'll keep nosin' around."

Sarah asked that he discover who spray painted the motorhome, and find out whether the rich Californian had displayed a bad temper. Harry said that Rosenbine played tennis every morning with another man at seven. When he told them which court the men played, they decided to watch the tennis match the following morning before rescuing Jenny from the kennel.

"We don't know his temperament," Dana said. "If he throws his racket when he loses a game, he might have killed Varina in a fit of anger."

Greg asked how Walter was faring. Dana smiled when she said he'd fired his nurse. That prompted Sarah to tell Harry about Walter's former caretaker, but a loud knock interrupted her description of Nurse Crabtree.

They were surprised to hear Rosie's graveled voice demanding to see Harry when Greg opened the door. Harry slid sheepishly from the dining nook and made his way there.

"You were supposed to have supper with me before we moved the trellis. What are you doing here?"

Harry turned to wave goodbye to Sarah before leaving. They could hear Rosie haranguing him all the way to her golf cart.

Sarah's face reddened. "Poor man. I wonder why he doesn't stand up for himself."

"He's probably putting up with her until he can find the suicide note," Dana said.

"What a nasty little woman she is. I'll bet she drove her husband to take his own life."

"He could have divorced her," Greg said. "There must be more to the story."

"Harry will discover what it is. He'd make a good detective. I just hope he doesn't get himself killed."

Greg asked if there were other suspects, including the director and his wife.

"The McKinseys?" Dana said she thought they were innocent.

"The husband is good looking," Sarah reminded her. "I'm sure Varina would have hit on him."

"She probably did and he rejected her."

Greg said he wouldn't rule out anyone at that point. "For all we know, it could have been a group project to get rid of Varina Zagori."

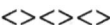

Dana reached to silence the alarm when it buzzed at six o'clock, wondering why Sarah had set it so early. She then remembered the tennis courts. Yawning, she missed awakening to the scent of freshly brewed coffee and Walter's smiling face. She wondered how he was getting along with his new nurse. It was only four o'clock in Sacramento, much too early to call.

"Sarah, time to rise and shine. Our tennis rackets await."

Sarah groaned and said she was too tired, but Dana insisted. "The morning air will refresh us and we might discover the killer's identity. Stan Rosenbine is high on my suspects' list. He had the most to lose and reminds me of a bull dog. I doubt he'd let a little con artist blackmail him for long."

Her sleuthing partner sat up in bed. "I don't think

he's the killer. There wasn't a golf bag in his cart, and I've never heard of anyone killed with a tennis ball."

"I thought most wealthy people played golf, but you could be right." Dana thought Rosenbine might have stashed his clubs somewhere after killing Varina. His corner lot provided enough undergrowth to hide more than one body as well as his golf bag. Was he registered as a golfer on the sheriff's list?

"Let's play a few sets of tennis while we watch for any signs of temper. Then we can permanently add or scratch Rosenbine from the list."

Sarah agreed as she slipped into a pair of white capris and tennis shoes. "Nothing like a strawberry smoothie and set of tennis to sharpen our investigative skills. We seem to be trawling in reverse lately. Too many suspects and not enough evidence."

"I'll try another people locator site when we get back. There must be more information online about our fellow residents."

Sarah made her way into the kitchen to dump frozen fruit into the blender. By the time they had gulped down their smoothies, Greg arrived, dressed in tennis togs, offering to drive them to the courts.

"I thought we could take turns watching the games while two of us play."

Once there, Sarah and Greg played a set while Dana sat on the sidelines. She watched Rosenbine's smooth delivery of the ball and noticed that he rarely missed a shot or serve. He seemed so self-assured that she wondered whether he ever lost his temper. If he'd planned to murder Varina, he either hired someone or carefully scheduled every move. He was definitely high on her suspects' list.

Sarah was red-faced and breathing heavily at the end of her match with Greg, and elected to sit out the next set. Dana felt that she already had enough evidence but didn't want to cause Rosenbine to suspect they were watching him. Greg easily won the set because she was so distracted.

During the drive home, Sarah asked if they had noticed a bulge at the waist of Rosenbine's shorts. Dana said no. Did Sarah think he was carrying a pistol while he played?

"Either that or he's wired for sound, which doesn't make sense."

"I'd like to know who his tennis partner is."

"Harry should know. I wonder whether he's suffered enough brow beating from Rosie by this time."

"He'll show up later and let us know, Sarah."

"Unless Rosie forbids it."

Dana laughed. "I don't think that tiny woman can control Harry. He may seem docile but I'm sure he has a temper."

"But not bad enough to kill someone."

Dana's mind raced back over all the suspects who could have committed the murder. The fact that Lacey and Camille had left their husbands and moved in together was still a shock. She wondered whether the sheriff knew. If he did, were they now high on *his* suspects list?

Sarah nudged her. "Time to pick up Jenny."

"While we're there, we can visit the RV dealership. I think repainting the motorhome will cost half as much as buying a new one. And we'd have to rent another RV while it's in the shop."

They noticed Harry's golf cart parked along the curb. They worried about his safety but knew how much he enjoyed his private sleuthing. They could always tell by his expression whether he had good news or bad. Unlike Greg, he had no poker face.

Grinning, Harry said, "Got somethin' here you might like to see." Glancing around the area, he said, "Maybe I'd better wait till we're all inside."

When they were seated, he pulled a five by seven framed photo from under his jacket and handed it to Sarah. "Does this guy look familiar?"

Sarah gasped and handed the picture to Dana. "It's either Bob's twin or his double."

"It certainly looks like him. If Bob *is* Rosie's son, it explains why he's been here. But why would she lie about him?"

"I'll ask Bob when he returns next week. In the meantime, why don't we check out the rest of our suspects online? I have a feeling that at least one of them has a police record—besides Rosie. Someone arrested for vandalism."

Harry's mouth was agape. "Rosie has a police record?"

Sarah told him about the assault charge and warned him not to incur Rosie's wrath. "It might be a good idea to stay away from her, Harry."

He shook his head. "I always wanted to be a detective and there appears to be more to this case than meets the eye. I'll just mosey on back over there to see what else I can find."

Sarah handed him the photograph and told him to put it back where he found it. Kissing his cheek, she warned him to be careful.

When he left, they showered and changed clothes before walking over to Greg's fifth wheel trailer. He then shepherded them into the backseat of his car. The tinted windows hid them from view and Dana knew that Sarah also appreciated their anonymity whenever they left home. Halfway to the main gate Sarah spotted two young boys examining a paint spray can. When she pointed them out to Greg, he pulled over and left the car to talk to them. Sarah rolled down her window to listen as their bodyguard held up the can for them to see.

"Black paint," he said, removing a handkerchief from his pocket to wrap the can. Turning back to the boys, he asked who owned the can. One of them said he'd found it in a dumpster.

"You weren't planning to spray paint an RV, were you?" Greg asked.

"No, sir," the taller boy said. "I was gonna paint my bike."

"Show me where you found the can."

The kid climbed on his bike and motioned them to follow. When he was back behind the wheel, Greg said, "If we're lucky, there might be more empty cans of paint in the dumpster, with fingerprints of the culprit. It could be a break in the case."

"Hurry," Sarah said. "The boy already turned the corner. He's a regular little speed demon."

They followed the boy down one street and turned another corner. They then spotted him parked beside a large dumpster at the service yard. Dana wondered how he had found the can in a dumpster nearly his own height.

Greg pulled alongside and got out. He asked when the boy had found the spray can and was told that morning. Greg rummaged through the trash and pulled out another can. Holding it between his thumb and index finger, he opened the car's trunk and placed both cans inside. Pulling out his wallet, he removed a couple of dollars, which he handed to the boy.

"Do you know who used these cans to spray paint a motorhome?"

The boy shook his head. "If I find out who done it,

I'll let you know."

Greg retrieved a business card and handed it to him, telling him where he was staying. "I'll make that ten dollars if you find out who painted the motorhome. But keep this confidential, just between the two of us. The person who used the cans is a criminal, so be careful."

The boy's happy grin revealed a missing tooth. Shaking hands with Greg, he mounted his bike and rode off.

"That was a piece of luck," Greg said. "The spray cans might be a coincidence, but I doubt many people use them in the resort. The cans may lead us to the killer."

Sarah gasped. "I hope we haven't placed the boy in danger."

"Whoever the killer is, he'd have a hard time catching him."

Dana agreed. The boy was already out of sight. She knew he would tell his friends, so it would evolve into a juvenile community search. A game not unlike a treasure hunt, although the killer was hardly a treasure.

Chapter Twenty

They planned to drop off the cans at the sheriff's office before retrieving Jenny from the kennel. The drive to town was a silent one with everyone immersed in their thoughts. When they reached the sheriff's office, Greg left them in the car while he hurried inside. He wasn't gone long. When he returned he said the lab would try to match the prints with those they had on file. They should know the results within a few days.

Sarah was relieved that they now had two methods of identifying the spray painter, who was undoubtedly the killer. She had originally empathized with whoever had killed Varina until the vandalism escalated into ruining the paint on their new RV. The murderer was not only vicious but possibly psychotic. Who among their suspects fit that pattern? She silently ran down the list, eliminating Jerome Zagori, Bob Grosler, the McKinseys, Paul Gates, and Rosie Darcun. That left the Dresslers, Lucy Gates, the Rosenbines, and Smiths. She leaned her head against the seat, a headache coming on.

When Greg's sedan pulled into the veterinary clinic parking lot, they all left the car to reclaim Jenny. The dog seemed happy to see them but barked as though scolding them for leaving her behind. Sarah led her out to the car while Dana paid the kennel bill.

On their way to the RV dealership, Greg said, "Too bad we can't let the dog sniff each suspect to determine the killer."

Dana remembered Jenny barking when she sniffed Bob's pants, but Sarah immediately came to his defense. "He said she barked because she smelled his dog. Jenny hasn't been around other dogs, so that has to be the reason."

"Maybe."

She knew her friend was unconvinced, but Dana didn't know Bob as well as she did. The poor man had been desperate to find another job and he had no reason to kill Varina. He didn't even know her.

Jenny jumped into Sarah's lap and licked her face. She wasn't a lap dog but she certainly was a lap full. Sarah gently pushed her down and stroked her head. Dogs, like people, would do almost anything for love. But love often drove people to revenge. Had any of Varina's victims actually been in love with her before she blackmailed them?

Jeffrey Dressler seemed to fit the category. Carrying around the greeting card from the victim must mean that he had actually been in love with her. Had his wife not known about the affair until she found the card? Or, if she had suspected the liaison, was the existence of the card the proof she needed to leave her husband? She and Lucy must have been good friends to suddenly leave their spouses to move in together. They obviously had discussed their cheating husbands long before deserting them.

She asked Greg if the sheriff knew about the deserting wives. He said he didn't know, but promised to call Sheriff Brandson when they returned to the resort. The sheriff would probably ask his suspects for bank statements to determine whether there had been large withdrawals from their accounts. Dressler must not have been blackmailed or he wouldn't be mourning Varina's death. He might be the man she was leaving her husband for.

She wished they could talk again with Camille Dressler, but doubted she would have anything to do with them. On second thought, Dressler wasn't rich. Why would Varina leave her husband for him instead of someone like Stan Rosenbine or the banker. Unless she was in love with him and had enough blackmail money stashed that she didn't need more. Sarah decided to write her suspicions down before she forgot them.

When they arrived at the RV sales lot, they found an identical motorhome to their present one, minus the graffiti. Asked if they took spray painted RVs as down payments on a new model, the salesman looked dubious. Shown a photo on Dana's smart phone, he said he would have to take a look in person, but that it would probably cost them a $25,000 trade-in deduction.

"Repainting a deluxe model is expensive, ma'am."

Dana sighed as she wrote down the address and lot number. Hopefully, her insurance would pay for part of the damage, but she had decided not to take possession of the new motorhome until the day they left for Wyoming. Agreeing to meet with him the following day, they left for the resort.

During the drive home they discussed their various suspects, hoping the killer wasn't someone they hadn't met. They also hoped the sheriff had the killer in his sites, along with more incriminating evidence than they had been able to unearth.

When they reached the resort and Greg parked his car in his own lot, they noticed a boy seated on his bicycle beside the fifth wheel trailer. Smiling, he nudged his kick stand into park and dismounted the bike. Before Greg had time to open his car door, the boy rapped on his window. When it was rolled down, the kid said, "Got your ten dollars ready?"

"Why, son? Do you know who bought the spray paint?"

"Yes, sir. One of my friends saw her throw the cans in the dumpster a couple of nights ago."

"A woman? Do you know her?"

"No, but she was driving a strange looking golf cart. It was after dinner and almost dark, so it was hard to tell who it was. But my friend said he would recognize the golf cart if he saw it again."

"You and your friend will get the money I promised plus a bonus if you can identify the woman," Greg said. "By the way, what's your name?"

"Josh."

Sarah thought, *Not another J,* She asked his parents' names.

"Jeff and Camille Dressler."

Good grief. That seemed to eliminate either one of them as the killer. Surely Josh's friend would have recognized Camille as the woman who tossed the cans in the trash—unless Camille and Lacey were partners in crime and Lacey had trashed the cans. There still seemed endless possibilities, although the chance there had been more than one person involved was becoming more plausible. Two women could have carried Varina to the lake and finished her off by drowning her. Then again, Camille seemed capable of carrying out the murder on her own. Lacey was much smaller and fragile so she would have needed help. Sarah was still convinced that Camille was the killer.

Sarah imagined both women sitting beneath a spotlight, the sheriff asking where they'd been on the night of the murder. She watched as Josh Dressler rode off on his bike to find his friend. They would probably canvas the resort, one street at a time, looking for the strange looking golf cart. She should have asked why the cart was strange so that they could locate it themselves.

"Let's feed Jenny," Dana said. "She appears to have lost some weight."

Sarah felt the dog's ribs. "You're right. She was either mourning our absence or her caretakers were afraid to feed her. I think that's the last time we take her to a kennel."

Jenny woofed as though she agreed.

There were several people standing at the curb gazing at the motorhome. They glared and turned to leave when she and Dana left the car. Good grief, did they actually believe *they* were the killers. Maybe they should trade the motorhome immediately and rent another until the case was solved.

Dana unlocked the coach, cringing at the red nail polish on the bottom of the door. "Maybe we should check to see if anyone wears this color. Whoever's leaving clues must be quite a game player or has a deep seated desire to be caught and punished for the murder."

"That's not a good reason to vandalize a brand new motorhome, Dana."

"You're right. We must have made the killer mad, which means we've talked to her."

"So you're still convinced it's a woman?"

"I don't think a man would go to such lengths, unless he has a mental problem. There's no logical reason for anyone to leave so many clues to incriminate us, unless Walter's right about the vandalism serving as a warning to stop our investigation."

Dana glanced at her watch and decided to call Walter. Sarah was also worried about him. She knew he'd put on a brave face for Dana, but was he actually out of danger? She cringed, knowing how difficult it had been for her friend to leave her husband. This case had to be wrapped up soon so they could all return to normal lives. She wasn't sure how their lives would change once Walter was living with them in the mansion, but it couldn't be worse than what they were currently experiencing.

Sarah listened to Dana's side of the conversation when they were seated in the motorhome. The call was brief and tears filled Dana's eyes when she clicked off.

"Walter's not doing well. He's in a lot of pain and didn't want to talk about it. He was gasping for breath and the nurse took the phone away from him."

"Sounds like he was shot in the lung."

"The doctor didn't tell me that, but you're probably right."

"Was it his former nurse, Dana?"

"No, it's an older nurse who's treating him like a son."

"That can't be all bad."

Dana bit her lip. "I need to talk to his doctor." Scrolling down her cell list, she punched in the number. A moment later, she said, "Doctor Seegraves is in surgery."

When someone knocked, Greg jumped up to answer the door. It was Harry, who lost his smile when he noticed Dana's tears. Sarah told him about Walter's condition and from his expression, she expected *him* to cry. Leading him outside, she pointed to the nail polish on the door and asked if he knew anyone who wore that color.

Wrinkling his forehead in thought, her cowboy said, "I've seen several women paint their toenails that color."

"Who?"

"Camille Dressler... Lacey Gates... Marie McKinsey... and Sylvia Koombs."

"The same color? Are you sure, Harry?" She hadn't considered the broker a suspect.

"Purdy sure. But red's red as far as I'm concerned."

Disappointed, Sarah took his arm and led him to the patio table, asking if he'd learned anything more about the suspects."

"Paul Gates has been burnin' up the phone wires tryin' to get his wife to come home."

"How do you know?"

"He was sittin' on his RV deck holdin' his ribs when I walked by. I stopped and talked to him."

"Did he act guilty in any way."

"He feels bad about his brief fling with Varina, but said when she found out he's near broke that she stopped seein' him."

"Was he mad about it?"

"No, I believe him when he says he was relieved it was over."

Varina must have had a new affair every week to have seduced so many men. But couldn't she tell that Paul Gates wasn't rich by the looks of his car and RV? And would Lacey kill Varina over a brief affair, knowing that Paul was only one of countless men in the resort? Camille Dressler was another story. Her husband must have had a serious affair and Camille discovered signs that he was planning to leave her. Better to have Varina dead and her husband jailed for murder, if she planned to frame him with the orange *J* ball. If not her husband, perhaps Jerome Zagori.

Sarah shivered at the cold bloodedness of the possible scheme. Then again, maybe Jeffrey Dressler was a serial womanizer and Camille had snapped after so much emotional abuse. The possibilities were endless.

"I gotta coupla pennies here for your thoughts, Miss Sarah."

"Sorry, Harry. I was just thinking about Paul Gates. I'm sure he learned his lesson but his wife may never forgive him."

"With him and his broken arm, I offered to cook some meals for him. I thought maybe you—"

"I'd be happy to take something over to him. I can't believe his wife left him in such terrible condition."

"Maybe that's her way of punishin' him."

"I hope you're right. She might go home when she hears the neighbors are pitching in to help him."

Harry cleared his throat. "I forgot to tell you that the Californians had a yellin' match."

"Stan and Alberta Rosenbine?"

"You could hear 'em all over the resort. Don't know what it was about, but she took off in her Mercedes and shoulda got a speedin' ticket."

"Maybe she found out about her husband agreeing to meet Varina in Hawaii."

"Could be. She must be stayin' someplace in town 'cause she didn't come back."

A divorce lawyer could make a fortune here in the resort. "Did you learn anything else?"

"No, but I'll keep snoopin'."

"Be careful. I'd never forgive myself if something happened to you."

"I'm carryin'," he said, lifting his jacket to show her his revolver."

She kissed him and sent him on his way, promising to deliver a casserole dish to Paul Gates that evening.

Greg and Dana looked up expectantly when she returned to the motorhome. Plopping down in her recliner, she relayed what Harry had said.

Dana smiled although there were still tear tracks on her cheeks. "Taking Paul Gates food is a good idea. It's not only neighborly, he may be feeling guilty enough to talk about Varina."

"Greg said, "He might tell us how she operated, which could open a door to something we haven't considered."

Sarah rose from her chair to survey the contents of the refrigerator. Pulling hamburger and veggies from storage boxes, she began to mix them together with tomato sauce. The sauce reminded her of blood and she shivered, wondering if there would be other murder victims before the case was resolved.

Chapter Twenty-One

Paul seemed grateful for the food and companionship. Inviting them in, he blubbered about his wife leaving. Dana hated to watch a grown man cry and took a seat beside him on the couch. Patting him on the back, she said, "You might feel better if you talk about Varina."

Taking out his handkerchief, he said, "She was a witch. I hate to speak ill of the dead, but she must have been Jezebel in a former life."

"How did she approach you?"

"She said she was leaving her husband and wanted to buy a lot on the other side of the resort. So I took her on a tour of the available properties. She then invited me to her lot for a drink. That evolved into several drinks and—you know."

"You wound up in her bed?"

He hung his head. "Nobody that good looking ever paid me any attention before and I was pretty looped by that time."

"How long was it before she tried to blackmail you?"

"The next day. I laughed because I thought she was

kidding. In this economy, realtors in an RV resort are near the bottom of the food chain."

"So what did she do?"

"She threatened to tell my wife. I told her I didn't have the money and that my wife would divorce me. She didn't care."

"So you killed her?"

"No!" He winced and held his ribs. "I figured that Lacey would forgive my one indiscretion."

"And did she?"

"I didn't tell her. It wasn't long before the wicked witch was dead, so I thought she wouldn't find out."

Dana asked how Lacey learned of the one-day stand.

"I'm not sure. When I came home from work three days later, Lacey was glaring at me. She asked if what she'd heard was true and I admitted my stupid mistake. She wouldn't tell me what she planned to do until she left to move in with Camille."

Sarah asked if Paul had received a greeting card signed *All my love, Varina*. He shook his head no. "She never said she loved me."

Dana asked if he had talked to Jeff Dressler about their wives moving in together. He said he'd tried but Jeff refused to talk about it. He seemed to be grieving Varina's death. "How could he grieve a witch's death?"

"Is there anyone who can help you while you recuperate?" Greg asked. "Friends or family members?"

"A few of the neighbors have stopped by but Lacey won't answer my calls." A tear slid down his cheek, causing a lump to form in Dana's throat.

"We'll talk to her, Paul. Take care and let us know if you need anything." Dana jotted down her cell number before they left.

"Well?" Sarah said when they were seated again in Greg's car. "Do you think Paul's telling the truth?"

"I do. And we need to talk to Lacey. A tragedy has happened and I'm not referring to the murder victim. Varina's disregard for others has gone a lot deeper than blackmail. She disrupted lives and whoever killed her saved countless people from heartbreak as well as bankruptcy."

"Are you saying the killer deserves a medal?"

"No, but you have to admit that Varina could have filled an entire courtroom with divorce cases. She had to have been psychotic to leave such a trail of unhappiness in her wake."

Sarah said, "Everyone agrees that it's a good thing she's dead but somebody has to pay the price. Do you think the killer will bump someone else off before this is over?"

"I doubt it. The killer, whoever she is, probably feels that's she's done a good deed and can't understand why we're trying to track her down. I agree with Walter that her vandalism is a means of warning us off the case."

"He or she may be panicking," Greg said. "Maybe the thinking was that because there are so many suspects that the killer will never be identified. Then you two started digging. I'm inclined to agree with Dana that it's a woman because of the types of vandalism committed. Men are usually more violent and destructive."

Sarah cleared her throat. "If that's true, we can cut our suspects' list in half. When shall we visit Lacey and Camille?"

Dana said there was no time like the present.

Their bodyguard thought otherwise, saying they needed to carefully plan their strategy. They reluctantly agreed. Dana was brimming with questions to ask their prime suspects, and knew Sarah was as well.

"Let's go home and write down our questions." Dana also wanted to place another call to Walter in private. He was never far from her mind.

Jenny was waiting for them, wagging a happy tail. Dana thought how simple a dog's life was. No worries about food, water, bills, dead bodies or killers lurking around the corner. She stooped to stroke Jenny's fur before pulling the cell phone from her purse. Taking the phone into the bedroom, she punched in the number to Walter's room. When he answered he sounded happy to hear her voice. She filled him in on all that had happened since their last call, and asked whether he agreed with Greg's theory that the killer was panicking.

"Why? What's happened, Love?"

She told him about the motorhome's graffiti and was shocked by his reaction

"I'll call Steve Brandson and ask him to allow you to leave. I can't recuperate while worrying about you."

"It's under control, Walter." *I shouldn't have told you.* Crossing her fingers, she said, "We think some kids painted the graffiti. I'm going to trade the old RV in on a better model."

"It's your money."

"There's no need to worry. Greg's a former sheriff's deputy so we're in good hands."

There was silence on the other end. She then heard a deep sigh. "You're a stubborn woman, Missus Grayson. I don't know what I'd do if something happened to you. Please keep that in mind."

"No heroics here, my dear. We're leaving everything to the sheriff." She hated to lie, but there was no need to worry him.

Next morning, after a round of smoothies, they set out for the Gates-Dressler fifth wheel trailer. They

found the two women still in their robes and anything but friendly. Greg stayed behind the wheel of his car while Dana and Sarah coaxed Lacey onto her patio.

"It's important that we talk to you," Dana said.

"If this is about my husband, you can save your breath."

"He's in bad shape, Lacey, and we're worried about him."

The petite blonde led the way to her patio table. Wrapping her robe tightly about her, she told them to make it quick. Her breakfast was getting cold.

Dana said, "Varina got him drunk on her patio and seduced him so she could blackmail him, Lacey. He was as much a victim of her schemes as she was of the killer's. He's so despondent that we're afraid he might do himself in."

Lacey hesitated a long moment before she said, "I'll drop over there this afternoon."

"Who told you about Paul and Varina?" Sarah asked.

"Camille."

"How did she know?"

"She said a friend watched Paul follow Varina into her trailer. She saw the overhang bounce for a while and waited till Paul left."

"Was he staggering?"

"She didn't say."

"You really need to talk to him," Dana said. "We know how hurt you are, but you should take the circumstances into consideration."

"How would you know how much he hurt me? Has it happened to you?"

"My husband ran off with a redhead," Sarah lied. "When he came back I forgave him. If he'd done it more than once I would have battered him with my baseball bat and thrown him out of the park."

Dana said, "Everyone deserves a second chance."

"I'll think about this." Rising resolutely from her chair, she walked to the trailer without looking back.

The two women hurried to Greg's car, finding him waiting expectantly.

"Did you get your answers?"

"Not entirely, but we hopefully convinced Paul's wife to talk to him."

"If Camille doesn't talk her out of it," Sarah said. "I'm sure she'll try. Misery does love company and I'll bet she doesn't want to stay here alone."

Dana thought they should probably take Paul another casserole dish that afternoon. They could ask if his wife had been there. Checking her watch, she said, "The RV salesman will be here in half an hour. We'd better go home."

They passed Harry who was taking his morning stroll. Waving, Sarah beckoned for him to follow. They were only half a block from home so they didn't stop to offer him a ride. His expression was gloomy so something must have happened.

Sarah waited for him when they left Greg's car. "What's wrong?"

"I'll tell you inside."

Once he was seated on the couch, Harry said, "Your friend Bob has returned like a homin' pigeon."

"Already? I thought he'd be gone for another week. When'd he get back?"

"Not long ago. I saw him takin' a suitcase outa his car while I was out walkin'."

"An RV salesman will be here any minute, Harry. We need to straighten things up."

Hanging his head, he said, "I knew you'd want me to leave when I told you."

Sarah handed him a duster and told him to make

himself useful. A moment later Bob appeared at their door. Sarah said she was glad to see him but asked that he return later. She explained about the salesman. He was obviously disappointed but three men in the motorhome was more than a crowd. And a dangerous one at that

"How about lunch?" Bob asked.

"You're on. I'll meet you at the restaurant at one o'clock."

Smiling, he left, and she turned to face a disheartened Harry, who said *he'd* planned to take her to lunch. Sighing, she realized that popularity had a price. "I'd rather have dinner with you, my dear. It's much more romantic. How about seven o'clock."

Handing her the duster, he managed a smile when he left for more sleuthing. Sarah knew she was going to have to choose between the two men before she found herself a nervous wreck.

"Greg and I will take another table at the restaurant for lunch," Dana said. "I know you think Bob's Mister Wonderful, but we're not going anywhere without a chaperone."

"You don't have to sit at the next table, Dana. Give us a little privacy."

"No problem. Just don't leave until we've finished lunch. Who knows where the killer's lurking. Maybe in the kitchen."

"Thanks for that, Dana. Now I'm afraid to order."

Greg smiled. "I think if the killer planned to kill either one of you, he would have done it before now."

The RV salesman arrived and they invited him in. Armed with a clipboard and pen, he began taking notes. Commenting on the interior's good condition, he said that someone had done a number on the RV's exterior.

"I'm afraid I'll have to discount your trade-in more than I had anticipated. Whoever spray painted your rig should be shot."

"We'll settle for arrested," Sarah said.

When the salesman left, Sarah hurried to change clothes for her lunch date with Bob. How could she decide between the two men? Dana's suspicions had her worried. What if her friend was right and one of them *was* the killer? She'd read about good-looking serial killers who charmed their victims and lured them to their deaths.

She realized she wasn't hungry.

Chapter Twenty-Two

Bob was waiting when Sarah arrived at the restaurant. His smile was wide as he stood to wave her to his table. Once she was seated, he leaned to plant a passionate kiss on her lips. She knew Dana and Greg would wait a few minutes before entering the restaurant, so she allowed the kiss to linger longer than she knew she should.

"I've missed you, Sarah. I hurried through my assignment so I could return sooner. I thought that after lunch we could take a drive into the country."

"To take pictures?"

"No, to give us some privacy." The expression on his face changed when Dana and Greg entered the restaurant.

"Sorry, Bob. I'm not allowed—"

"So I see. Your shadows are here to protect you. I thought you trusted me."

Sarah smiled. "I do trust you, Bob. Dana and Greg decided to take advantage of today's blue plate special."

"Then you'll take the drive with me?"

"No. We agreed that neither of us would go anywhere without the other." She then told him about the brake punctures and Dana's injury. "And speaking of injuries, how's your head?"

He waved the question aside. "How am I going to court you if we're never alone."

"Court me? I haven't heard that term in years."

"You know my intensions, Sarah. I can't wait for forever."

"I'm sorry to hear that. Dana's husband waited for her for years. That's true love."

"Husband? I thought she was single."

"We have a lot of catching up to do."

After they had ordered their meals, she told him about the shooting and their trip to Sacramento.

"It's not safe for you and your friend to investigate the murder, Sarah. Whoever killed the Zagori woman might decide to kill you too."

"He would have done it by now... By the way, why didn't you tell me your mother lives in the resort?"

"What makes you think my mother—?"

"A friend noticed your picture in her motorhome."

Bob groaned. "They say everyone has a double."

"True, but they're not all as handsome as you."

His uneven smile caused a cold chill to race down Sarah's spine. He hadn't denied that Rosie was his mother. Why didn't they want anyone to know they were related? Then again, maybe Harry was wrong about them. There was still the chance that Harry was trying to get rid of his competition.

When Bob finished telling her about his trip, Sarah placed her napkin on her plate and thanked him for lunch. Appraising Dana and Greg from the corner of her eye, she noticed they had finished their meals and seemed to be waiting for her. Rising from her chair so quickly that it nearly fell, she said goodbye before Bob had a chance to ask for another date. Trembling, she realized that she was afraid of him.

Dana and Greg followed her and tailgated the golf cart back to the motorhome. When they were all seated in the dining nook, Sarah told them about her fears. "I'm not as good at appraising people as you are, Dana, but the way Bob looked at me as I was leaving gave me chills. There's something sinister about that man."

Dana quizzed her about their conversation. What had he said and why did it bother her?

"He wants to court me. Can you believe that?"

"Yes, you're an attractive woman."

Sarah snorted. "I'm thirty pounds overweight and we hardly know each other."

"So you think he's coming on too strong, too soon?"

"Absolutely. You should have seen his expression when I asked him if he were Rosie's son?"

"He denied it?"

"Not exactly, Dana. He avoided the question."

"I was watching his body language and thought he was guarded. We were too far away to hear what he was saying. I'm sorry, but I may be prejudice against him because of his lie. After watching him, I don't think he has an honest bone in his body."

"This may surprise you but I'm now inclined to agree."

Greg, who had been silent until then, said, "Looks like Bob Grosler has permanently moved over to our suspects' column."

Sarah nodded, feeling a deep sense of sadness. "For the life of me, I can't understand how he became involved with Varina so soon after he arrived. He said he had only been in the resort a couple of days before we got here."

"He's a liar," Dana said. "We should have realized that he can't tell the truth about anything."

You mean that this lonely widow was duped by his charm and good looks. But you're too nice to say it. "I forgot to mention that he wanted to take me for a drive in the country."

Dana's hand flew to her chest. "Thank heavens you were too smart to fall for that. We might never have seen you again."

Sarah nodded in agreement. "Shall we tell the sheriff what we suspect, Greg?"

"Not quite yet. Let's see what Harry comes up with in the next couple of days."

"I'm worried about Harry. The killer must know by now that he's snooping and telling us what he's discovered."

Dana said, "I should probably hire *him* a bodyguard."

Greg nodded. "Not a bad idea, but it would certainly put a crimp in his sleuthing."

Sarah felt a lump form in her throat. "Then how can we protect the dear, sweet man?"

Greg offered to have a talk with Harry the next time he came to visit. There were ways that he could protect himself, other than carrying a gun.

It was time to make a casserole dish for Paul Gates. A broken arm and ribs were handicaps enough, let alone trying to feed himself in a trailer. How he got dressed and made himself meals was beyond Sarah's comprehension. She was ready to turn Lacy over her knee if she didn't forgive him. She then thought of Camille Dressler, her prime suspect. If *she* were the killer, there was no way that she would allow Lacey to return home. Sarah tented her hands and prayed that Lacey was at home with Paul at that very moment.

Once the casserole was baked and cooling on the

counter, Sarah asked if they thought it was safe to accept Harry's dinner invitation.

"What if Bob comes to the restaurant while you're there?" Greg asked. "That could cause a scene and maybe even a fight. He'd also know that Harry's your informant."

"We'd better go to a restaurant in town."

Dana was worried the killer might have tampered with Harry's brakes. "I think we'd all better go to town together in Greg's car, don't you?"

"That will disappoint Harry but I'm sure he'll understand." Sarah lifted her tuna casserole with hot pads and placed it on a tray. "Let's take this over to the Gates trailer and hope for the best."

It was only a three minute drive and they were pleased to find the Gates golf cart parked on the lot although the car was missing. Lacey must have gone home. Sarah knocked at the door and waited. When no one answered, she set the casserole dish on the top step and tried the door. It wasn't locked and she peered inside, calling both Paul and Lacey. She waited a full minute before setting the box with the casserole dish inside the door.

When she reached Greg's car she was troubled. "Should we go inside to see if they're all right? I can't imagine Paul driving himself anywhere. And I know that Lacey had possession of the golf cart. She had to have been here."

"Don't panic," Greg said. "Maybe Lacey decided to drive Paul somewhere and they left the golf cart behind."

Dana suggested they call security. Retrieving her cell phone, she scrolled down the screen until she found the number. When the security guard answered, she was relieved that it wasn't the grumpy man she had talked to the night of the swimming pool note. He didn't seem concerned but said he would be there within half an hour.

"Half an hour? They could be dead before then."

"Not to worry, ma'am. I'll get there as soon as possible."

They waited in Greg's car while Sarah worried about her date with Harry. Would he think she stood him up if he found them not at home? And where were the Gates?"

Greg suggested that she call Harry.

"He never gave me his number. We need to get the owner's directory to look him up."

"And Lacey and Paul's cell numbers," Dana said. "We may be making a big fuss over nothing."

They decided to rush home before the security guard arrived. Back at the motorhome they found Harry sitting at the patio table drinking a glass of wine. "I knew you'd be here sooner or later," he said. "I hope you don't mind that I borrowed some wine from your outdoor cooler."

"Are you celebrating or mourning something, Harry?" Sarah asked.

"Both. I'm mournin' the fact that Bob Grosler stole my girl—"

"No, he didn't. I'm not seeing him again."

Harry's face lit up like a neon sign.

"Now that's settled, what are you celebrating?"

"I have some news for you."

Dana left the motorhome with the directory in hand. "Let's go. Harry, come with us."

When they were seated in Greg's car, Sarah asked again why Harry was so happy.

"Rosie finally admitted that Bob Grosler's her son."

"Did she say why she had denied him?"

"I took a bottle of my best bourbon to loosen her tongue, and she finally admitted he's a criminal. He spent six years in the cross bar hotel for assault and armed robbery."

Sarah gasped. "Then why didn't that information turn up when Dana researched him online."

"He changed his name when he got outa prison."

Sarah felt faint. Why had Bob wanted to court her and take her for a drive in the country? To stop her from investigating Varina's death by killing her? No wonder he seemed disappointed that Dana had married. He probably wanted to court her as well.

"But how did he know Varina?"

"I didn't think to ask, but I'll find out tomorrow."

Greg warned him again to be careful. He might get himself killed.

The security guard arrived moments after they reached the Gates lot. They waited in the car while he went inside the trailer to look around. When he closed the door, he told them that nothing seemed out of place and there was no sign of a struggle.

Greg thanked him and said that he would call the sheriff's office to notify them of the missing couple. They then returned to the motorhome to dress for dinner. Sarah knew the others had the Gates couple on their minds. She hoped that they had gone for a drive to talk things over, and were already home.

They drove past the Gates trailer on their way out of the resort. The car was still missing and Greg decided to call the sheriff. After a few minutes wait, Steve Brandson came on the line. Sarah listened intently as Greg described the Gates' circumstances. He also filled Brandson in on Bob Grosler's prison sentence. When Greg asked, neither Dana nor Sarah remembered the man's first name listed as Rosie Darcun's relative, but agreed his last name was Darcun.

"I wonder who the sheriff was planning to arrest for the murder," Dana said as they drove from the resort. "It sounded as though an arrest was imminent when he called me in Sacramento."

Greg frowned. "Steve and I are friends but he didn't mention an arrest to me. Maybe he changed his mind and wants to investigate the case more thoroughly. He's tied up with four other cases, something that's never happened on his watch. Or for that matter, during the twenty-five years I was with the department."

Sarah asked if Greg thought the murders were connected in some way.

"It's very probable although the murders were committed in different parts of the county."

"But were the bodies all found in rural areas?"

Greg said, "All were found in water. A stream, reservoir, drainage ditch, and river."

Both women gasped.

Dana asked, "Did they all drown or did they die from blows to the head?"

"The victims were middle aged women. Two of them died before they hit the water, the Zagori woman was the last."

Dana turned to face Sarah in the back seat. "Are you thinking what I'm thinking?"

"Bob must have killed them," Sarah said, gripping the front of her blouse. "He might have killed more women while he was supposed to be away on assignment... I think I'm going to be sick."

Greg pulled off the side of the road and Harry helped Sarah from the car. Supporting her while she retched, Harry handed her his handkerchief and then hugged her. When they again took their seats, Greg asked if Sarah wanted to return home. She said no. She didn't want to ever return to Paradise Acres. The thought of kissing a serial killer had left an indelible scar on her soul. She knew she'd never get over it.

"Okay, ladies, where would you like to eat tonight?"

"The Horizons," Sarah said. She envisioned the indoor waterfall and Polynesian atmosphere. It was the perfect place to forget all that had happened, at least temporarily. Just thinking about Bob Grosler—Darcun or whatever his name was— made her queasy. She wanted to spend a pleasant evening with Harry. Dana wouldn't mind if they sat at their own table near the waterfall. She had seen a televised commercial of the restaurant a few nights earlier, and thought the place was just south of heaven.

The parking lot was crowded. Sarah still felt a bit nauseated but wasn't one to turn down an exotic meal. A small table near the waterfall was unoccupied and she led Harry there. A hostess soon arrived to sputter about not allowing them to seat themselves, but Sarah waved her away. If the table was reserved, let them find somewhere else to dine. Smiling at Harry, she said, "I don't know what we would have done without your fearless sleuthing."

He beamed and reached across the table to take her hand. "I always wanted to be a detective but I inherited my parents' cattle ranch so my life was already laid out for me."

"You're a good detective, Harry, but I'm still worried about you."

Someone sat down at a table behind Harry, causing her heart to lurch. *Bob! What's he doing here? He must have followed us into town. Should I tell Harry? And where are Dana and Greg seated?* Sarah felt frozen in place, unable to speak or move. She avoided eye contact with Grosler, aka Darcun, although he waved to her. He was alone and dressed in a charcoal suit with a crimson tie. His looks would have made her swoon if she didn't suspect him of killing middle aged women.

Dana and Greg must have seen him by now. Would either one of them come to the table to talk to her? She felt as though she were going to heave again but still couldn't move.

"What's wrong, Miss Sarah? Are you gettin' sick?"

She shook her head no. She didn't want to ruin his evening. The waitress returned with menus, asking if they would like to order something to drink. Sarah opened her menu and pointed to a bottle of red wine. She didn't notice the brand and didn't care. She just needed more than a sip of spirits to brace her for what she feared was to come. She couldn't tell if Darcun was carrying a gun.

Please, Dana and Greg, come to our rescue.

A young waitress arrived with a bottle of champagne. "A gift from the gentleman seated at the table behind you."

Sarah looked up to see Darcun smiling at her. "I refuse his gift. Take it back to him."

Harry half rose in his chair when he noticed their benefactor. Sarah grasped his arm and told him to ignore Darcun. "Don't let him ruin our evening."

"I'm afraid he already has. I'll ask the waitress to seat us somewheres else."

"It's all right, Harry," she whispered. "He doesn't know what we know about him. He's just making a nuisance of himself, trying to ruin my evening out with you."

"I'm packin' so he'd better watch his peas and ques."

Sarah gazed at the waterfall and sighed. She'd gone so long without a man in her life. Now she had two men fighting over her, one of them a suspected killer. The same waitress approached with a bottle of red wine and Harry insisted she seat them elsewhere.

"I'm afraid we're filled to capacity," the waitress said, but I'll reseat you as soon as there's a vacancy."

When she left, Sarah asked if Harry had spotted their companions.

"Behind you, two tables over and to your left. They seem to have noticed Bob and motioned for us to ignore him."

"Then let's enjoy our dinner and each other. There are three guns against one if he's carrying, and I don't think he'll start anything in the restaurant."

Chapter Twenty-Three

"Isn't that Grosler-Darcun seated behind the happy couple?" Greg said a moment after they had ordered their dinners.

"You're right, it is. What should we do?"

"I'll call Steve Brandson from the alcove. Signal me if Darcun approaches Sarah."

Dana nodded and pretended to study her menu. Watching covertly as Sarah refused the champagne, she noticed the murderous expression on Darcun's face. Would he try to grab Sarah and drag her to his car? The four of them should have sat together, but her friend wanted time alone with Harry. She glanced over at the alcove where Greg was still talking on his cell. Rubbing her elbow over the revolver hidden in her waistband, she planned which actions to take if Darcun approached either Sarah or Harry.

From the corner of her eye Dana noticed Greg leave the alcove and make his way back to the table. He wasn't smiling. When he took his seat, he said, "Steve's investigators haven't had time to do a thorough background check on Darcun, so he's not ready to make an arrest."

"We need to keep a close eye on Sarah *and* Harry. I don't think alias Bob is the type to put up with competition for long. Thank heavens he's not aware that we know about his criminal record."

"Darcun must already know about his mother's confession to Harry. Unless she's afraid to tell him."

"If he does know, he's out to get Harry as well."

"I don't think we have to worry about that tonight, Dana. He must have seen us sitting here and realized the odds are against him. Harry can bunk with me until we figure out a way to protect him."

"Good idea. I'm afraid Harry's snooping days are over. If he's come too close to the truth, he's a likely candidate for the morgue."

When the waitress approached with their dinner, Greg said to enjoy her meal. He would keep an eye on Darcun. "If he's planning anything, he'll do it while he thinks we're distracted."

Dana lowered her head and watched their suspect through her lashes. She noticed him glance their way and glared at him to let him know that he was under surveillance. Averting his eyes, he took a long gulp of the rejected champagne and studied his menu. It was going to be a long, drawn out dinner that Dana anticipated would end with antacids.

She could smell the lobster and steak when it was placed before her, and thanked the waitress without glancing up. Sarah and Harry had Darcun's full attention, like a rattlesnake lying in wait for its prey. Dana shivered, hoping the lobster wouldn't stick in her throat.

<><><>

Harry reached to pat Sarah's hand. "You're not eating. Why don't we switch chairs so you don't have to look at that varmint?"

"That would make it easier for him to grab me, Harry."

"If he tries, I'll hogtie him and throw him on the floor. In case I didn't mention it, I was a champion bulldogger and steer wrestler in my day."

Sarah smiled. "I think I love you, Harry."

"I know I love you, Miss Sarah. If we weren't in this present situation, I'd get down on one knee to propose to you."

"And I'll probably accept. But tomorrow's soon enough."

"Probably? You have to think about it?"

Sarah leaned forward to whisper, "There's a serial killer sitting at the next table and I don't think he'd be happy to hear me accept your proposal."

Harry nodded. "I can wait."

Bob left his table to walk over. Sarah gasped when he placed a hand on Harry's shoulder. "Mind if I join my fellow resort mates?" he said.

Sarah was suddenly aware that Greg was standing beside her, towering over Darcun. "Let's make it a dinner party, shall we, Bob? Pull up a chair. I have some questions for you."

Darcun backed away, saying, "I think I'll finish my meal first, if you don't mind."

"Not at all. I'm sure Miz Cafferty would enjoy having dinner alone with her fiancé."

Sarah glanced down at the small black velvet box sitting next to Harry's plate. Why hadn't she noticed it sooner? She knew why. She had been watching Darcun and the waterfall when she should have been focusing on Harry.

"Fiancé?" Darcun said. "Then why did you have lunch with me?"

"Harry hadn't asked me yet."

Darcun said nothing more as he returned to his table. Glancing up at Greg, Sarah mouthed, "Thank you."

"Why don't you join us at our table?" Greg said. "I'll keep an eye on Square Pants while you enjoy your meals."

They reluctantly followed him to the table where Dana anxiously awaited them. Standing, she hugged Sarah and asked that she sit next to her. "What's this?" she asked, indicating the small velvet box.

"An engagement ring. I planned to ask Miss Sarah to marry me tonight, but she insists that I wait till tomorrow."

"I changed my mind, Harry. You can propose to me properly tonight at home."

Harry appeared so happy that Sarah knew she couldn't reject his proposal, although she doubted she was ready.

"Come to the ladies' room with me," Dana said "I don't think either one of us should go alone."

Once there, they sat in a small lounge where Dana took her hand. "Are you sure this is what you want? You haven't known him long."

"I don't want to hurt him and I think I'm in love."

"Is it because I married Walter?"

"No, I want to get married again."

"Have you talked about where you'll live?"

"Harry likes to travel. He owns four RV lots around the country."

"Are you sure that's what *you* want?"

Sarah twisted her fingers. "I don't know, Dana. I'm scared."

"Let's go back to the table. If I were you, I'd tell Harry that you need more time to get acquainted."

When they returned to the table, Sarah noticed that Darcun had disappeared. When she asked where he'd gone, Greg said he'd followed him to the parking lot and watched him drive away.

"I hope he doesn't do something underhanded," Greg said. "More vandalism or another murder."

Sarah wondered if Darcun had spray painted the motorhome and planted the lingerie in their golf bags. Greg said he wouldn't put it past him. He had talked to Harry in their absence about guarding the two women around the clock until the killer was apprehended.

"I've got a fifty foot lariat," Harry said. "I'll hogtie the critter if he gets anywhere near you."

Sarah breathed a sigh of relief. "We'll feel a lot safer knowing you two are standing by. But what should we do if Bob knocks on our door?"

"Don't open it," Greg said. "Harry will stand guard during the day and I'll keep watch at night. If Darcun's foolish enough to show up—"

"We'll send him packin'," Harry said.

Sarah pushed her plate aside. "Now that's settled, what about Lacey and Paul Gates?"

"The sheriff has issued an alert. They've hopefully been located by now."

"I wouldn't put it past Camille to make them both disappear or maybe she and Lacey are still in cahoots."

"If they are, Jeff Dressler's also in danger."

Since no one seemed in the mood to finish their meals, Dana suggested they return to Paradise Acres. First stop, the Gates fifth wheel trailer.

<>< ><>

The trailer was still dark and the car missing when they pulled onto the Gates lot. Maybe Paul had returned and gone to bed early. But where was Lacey? Dana suggested they stop at Lacey and Camille's rental trailer. They found it also dark although it was only a quarter past nine. Lacey's car wasn't there, only Camille's fancy golf cart. She wondered who Josh was living with, his mom or dad. She also wondered if he'd come to Greg's trailer with information about the women who tossed the spray cans into the dumpster. There were still too many loose ends to tie the murder case into a secure knot.

Should they drive over to Jeff Dressler's RV to talk to him? Greg thought it best to wait until morning, after he'd had a few hours' sleep. He said he'd first check to see if Josh had left a note. Dana wondered whether the boy had told his mother about Greg's offer, which could have led to the Gates' disappearances. Was Camille Dressler missing too? That was one mystery they'd have to solve soon.

There was also the matter of Harry's proposal. Was Sarah going to accept? With Harry around all day, it would be difficult to refuse him. Dana approved of Harry but she couldn't imagine not seeing Sarah on a regular basis. When Walter left the hospital and retired, life would never be the same. Calling Walter was her first priority when they reached the motorhome.

Greg insisted on inspecting the RV before he allowed them to enter. Jenny was barking and he handed Sarah the leash, so that she and Harry could take the dog for a short walk. Sarah took her bat and was warned to watch for movement in the shadows. Dana was relieved when they returned not long afterward.

Sarah was excited. "We just saw Camille pull onto her lot. We waited to see if she was alone and I don't think she noticed us. She was carrying something that looked like a body bag."

Dana sat down hard in her recliner. There were too many suspects. They had concluded that Bob Grosler, alias Darcun, was the killer. Could he have formed a partnership with Camille Dressler? That seemed too farfetched to believe. Camille was six feet tall and Darcun was vertically challenged, no taller than five feet six. They were both strong willed and would probably kill each other during an argument. Stranger pairings have happened but the two of them simply didn't constitute a match.

If Darcun *was* in partnership with Camille, why was he hitting on Sarah, unless he was planning to rid himself of all the witnesses? That would mean that he was intending to kill her as well. No wonder he was disappointed that she had married. It would make it more difficult to lure her for a ride into a rural area. Dana shivered at the thought.

They gathered in the dining nook while Sarah brewed them a pot of coffee. When she had poured them each a cup, she said, "We completely forgot about the woman Varina was playing golf with the day we arrived. Her face was shaded by her golf cap but she was about Varina's size. Harry had said that Varina only had one woman friend. She must have the answers they needed to solve this case unless she had been killed too."

Greg took out his cell phone to call Sheriff Brandson. When the sheriff picked up, Greg asked for the names of the murder victims. Dana reached for a pen to write them down as Greg repeated them: Liz Bellsworth, Terri Checkolosky, Carolina Simson, and Michelle Starone. Harry groaned as he pointed to the list.

"Liz Bellsworth lived here till a coupla weeks ago," he said. "She was Varina's friend."

"Was she married?"

"She was a widow."

Sarah's expression soured. "That explains why they were friends. Liz didn't have a husband for Varina to seduce."

"She did but he died a coupla months ago."

"About the same time as Rosie's husband?"

"They died a week apart, as I recall."

"Did he also kill himself?" Dana asked.

"Not to my knowledge. If he did, Liz kept it a secret."

"That puts a whole new spin on things," their bodyguard said when his call ended. "I know that Steve thinks the murders are somehow connected. Liz Bellsworth's friendship with Varina Zagori may be the link we've been searching for."

Harry told them all he knew about the Bellsworths and that he wondered why a nice lady like Liz had formed a friendship with Varina.

Dana speculated that Varina didn't have any female friends and that Liz felt sorry for her.

"All I know is that she disappeared a few days before you found Varina's body. Her motorhome is still here and I thought she had gone to visit her son in Oregon." He reached into his pocket and withdrew his wallet.

"I think I have a picture of Liz, Ben and me here somewheres."

Sarah asked if they had been friends.

"I used to go fishin' with Ben," he said. Pulling the photograph from a plastic holder, he held it for the others to see.

Sarah reached for the picture and shrieked. "The vest! She's wearing the vest." She handed the photo to Dana.

"I think you're right, Sarah." Rising from the dining nook, Dana pulled a magnifying glass from a kitchen drawer. Holding it near the images, she said, "If it's not *the* gray vest, it's a duplicate."

Harry appeared puzzled. "What vest?"

Sarah told him about discovering the vest in the motorhome's storage compartment. She asked if he had seen anyone else wearing one like it.

Shaking his head, Harry denied knowing of any others. "Liz wore that vest a lot. She said she grew up in Sharpsburg, near the Antietam Battlefield in Maryland, and was a Civil War buff."

"Thank heavens," Sarah said. "One mystery's solved. But now we have to contend with five murders instead of one."

Greg took the photograph and examined it. "Not necessarily. One or more could have been copycat murders."

"Back to square one," Dana said, holding her head in her hands. "Nothing about this case makes sense."

Harry grinned. "It does if you consider the case upside down and backwards."

Chapter Twenty-Four

Puzzled, Sarah wondered what Harry meant. She imagined herself standing on her head to contemplate the murders.

He grinned. "We need to look at the murders from different angles. Who wanted Varina dead more than anybody else?"

Sarah sighed, telling him they had already discussed the suspects' motives for killing the Zagori woman. Did Harry have information he hadn't shared?

"I was thinkin' it's strange that four other women were killed and left in different kindsa water. Not a lake like Varina."

"Maybe the killer has a fresh water fetish or is simply trying to confuse the investigators."

Greg said, "The first four victims were strangled before they were dumped in the water. Varina was hit in the head with a golf ball. What does that tell you?"

Dana sat upright. "It probably means that Varina's killer was a copycat murderer who didn't know how the other women died. Only that their bodies were found in water. He or she assumed that Varina's murder would be attributed to the same person."

Greg nodded. "The murders happened over a five week period and the sheriff's checking on the whereabouts of all the suspects during that time."

Sarah grimaced. "That eliminates Bob as a suspect He was in Venezuela last month."

"He might have lied about his whereabouts," Dana said.

Greg reminded them that he had checked with the office receptionist about Bob's arrival. "Darcun told the truth about getting here two days ahead of you. And the receptionist didn't recall him staying here before."

"Imagine that. Bob told the truth about *something*." Sarah's sarcasm surprised Dana.

"Maybe he stayed in another RV park before he came here."

"It's possible," Greg said. "He could have been concerned about his mother living alone after his father died."

"Then why didn't he attend the funeral?" Dana asked.

Harry scowled. 'I don't think Rosie's going to tell me why. I'm sure Bob told her not to have anythin' else to do with me."

Sarah patted his arm. "You've done enough. I'm worried about your safety."

They had stirred up a hornet's nest by investigating the murder without considering the consequences. Dana probably wouldn't have married Walter if she hadn't asked for his help. But it had endangered all their lives, including her husband's and Harry's.

"Better check on the Gates couple," Dana said. "And report that Sarah and Harry saw Camille carrying what looked like a body bag out of her trailer tonight."

Greg slid from the nook and walked into the living area to call Sheriff Brandson. Dana strained to hear Greg's side of the conversation as Sarah and Harry whispered in the background. When Greg clicked off, he sat down heavily on the couch, apparently deep in thought. Sitting next to him she heard Jenny bark when someone tapped at the door. Dana heard a young voice when Greg went to answer. She recognized the voice as the Dressler boy's and told Greg to invite him in. Motioning for Josh to be seated, Dana asked why he was out so late at night.

"Mom's not home," he said. "And I don't know where Dad is. We don't live with him anymore."

Dana wanted to hug the boy but sat back as Greg questioned him about the mysterious golf cart.

"It's gone, sir. Me and my friend Sam looked at every lot but couldn't find it." His lips trembled and Dana thought he would cry.

Greg pulled out his wallet and handed him two five dollar bills, telling Josh that he appreciated his efforts. He also asked that he and his friend continue to watch for the golf cart, which could be hidden in a lot shed or taken into a shop for repairs. He was then asked where his mother might have gone. The boy shrugged, admitting that she was rarely home anymore.

Dana groaned inwardly, concerned about him. What was Camille thinking, leaving Josh alone at night? She thought to ask about Lacey and Paul Gates. Had he seen them? Not since that morning, the boy said, when Lacey left in her golf cart. He hadn't seen Paul since he returned from the hospital.

Greg offered to drive him home but the boy refused. His bike was outside and he didn't want to leave it there. Greg decided to follow him back to the trailer. Returning some fifteen minutes later, their bodyguard said he had swung by the Gates' lot and found their car still missing.

"No lights in the trailer?" Dana asked.

"Dark as deep hole. I hope Steve's deputies have located the Gates couple by now. I hated to leave Josh alone at the rental lot. No telling when his mother will return."

"You don't think that—?" Dana paused, wondering if Camille had been killed along with Paul and Lacey Gates. Or had Camille tossed both Gates in a river somewhere? She envisioned Paul trying to fight off the woman with his broken arm and ribs. Maybe she had convinced Lacey that her husband deserved killing.

"Camille musta left home right after Miss Sarah and I saw her carryin' that bag into the trailer," Harry said from the dining nook. "She seemed in a hurry."

If it *was* a body bag, Dana thought, would she hide it in the trailer? That seemed too risky.

Sarah insisted that Camille was the killer, but Harry shook his head, apparently still convinced the former nurse was innocent.

Whipping out his cell phone, Greg again called Sheriff Brandson, apologizing for the late hour. When he clicked off, he said, "The Gates' car has been found."

"Where?" the others asked in concert.

"North of here. Just over the county line." He answered the question before anyone could ask: "No bodies were found."

Sighing with relief, Dana asked if that meant that law enforcement in both counties were on the case. He nodded in the affirmative. "An APB has been issued in surrounding states as well."

"Has one been issued for Camille Dressler?"

"I believe so. Fortunately, investigators have the descriptions and license plate numbers of all the suspects' vehicles."

Sarah left the dining nook to stand over them. "What about Josh? Can we bring him here to stay with us?"

"If his mother doesn't show up by morning, I'm sure relatives will be notified to pick him up. Or child services."

"What about his father?"

"Dressler might be the killer, Miss Sarah. When I drove by he wasn't home."

"I doubt that a man who carries a greeting card around would kill the person who signed it with love."

"This is a fine kettle of crawdads," Harry said to himself. "Just when I think I've got it all figured out, somebody tosses me another fishin' net."

Greg told everyone to stay calm. The sheriff promised to call with further news. In the meantime, Greg would drive back to see about Josh and suggest that he stay with a friend. Harry would stand guard while he was gone.

"How in heaven's name could one person cause so much heartache and trauma?" Sarah asked no one in particular.

"Selfishness and greed," Dana muttered. "Varina was obviously a sociopath."

"More déjà vu. Remember Lori Murphy? The young woman we found dead on the Arizona Interstate, who thought she was God's gift to men?"

Dana sighed. "How could I forget? *Her* goal was breaking up relationships, not blackmailing wealthy men."

"A deadly practice all the same."

Someone rapped at the door. They waited, expecting Greg to appear. When the door didn't open, Harry drew his revolver and pushed down the latch. When the door opened, they heard him say, "Get your ass outa here, Darcun. You're not welcome."

"Sarah," Darcun called. "May I have a minute to talk to you?"

Sarah seemed frozen in place, unable to move, so Dana went to the door instead. "Sarah's not feeling well. You'll have to come back tomorrow."

"But it's important that I speak to her tonight."

"I'm sorry but—"

"It's all right, Dana," her friend said from somewhere behind her. "I have a few questions for Mister Darcun."

Turning back to face her, Dana whispered, "Not until Greg gets back."

Sarah nodded. Leaning around Dana and Harry, she told him to return the following morning at nine. Surprising them all, he turned to leave.

It seemed an eternity before Greg returned, his expression gloomy. He reported that he had driven the boy to his friend Sam's motorhome and received permission for him to stay the night. Their mothers were friends so it wasn't a problem, although Sam's mother had peppered him with questions about Camille's whereabouts. No one seemed to know where either of Josh's parents were. Maybe they were together. Hopefully, one hadn't killed the other.

Greg wondered why Darcun had stopped by, unless it was to lure Sarah into his car. Sarah visibly shivered when she said she was afraid he would try to break into the motorhome that night.

"I'll be sitting watch here in the RV. If I happen to nod off, Jenny will let me know that someone's around." Greg leaned to affectionately pet the dog.

Sarah's cell phone rang and she scrambled to retrieve it from the dining nook. "It's Bob. Shall I answer it?"

Greg told her to find out what he had to say but not to agree to meet him anywhere. They all gathered around her as she lifted the phone to her ear. Dana watched her facial expressions, which evolved from scowling to a slight smile. What was he telling her? And did she believe him?

Chapter Twenty-Five

Sarah slid into the dining nook following the call. "You're not going to believe this. Bob saw Camille herding the Gates couple into their car at gunpoint after dark. He said they drove off with Lacey at the wheel."

Greg asked if he had reported it to the sheriff.

"He didn't say. But he kept telling me that he wants to hold me in his arms to protect me from the killer."

Harry's face was crimson. Swearing beneath his breath, he reached to hug Sarah. "No forked tongue paparazzi's gonna touch my lady."

"Not to worry," she said. "There's no way that man will get his hands on me."

Greg made another call to Sheriff Brandson to report the incident. "I don't know whether Darcun's lying, but I thought you should know what he had to say."

"Why would Camille kill the Gates couple? It doesn't make sense," Dana said. "Unless she wants the sheriff to think Paul and Lacey committed the murders and decided to escape."

"Or maybe Camille wanted it to appear that Lacey

killed her husband because of his affair."

"All the wives are suspects," Sarah said. "Especially Camille. The sheriff knows about Dressler's affair and the greeting card his investigators must have confiscated."

"Unless Camille destroyed it."

Dana snapped her fingers. "If it wasn't so late, I'd call Walter to ask if Camille tore up the card when she found it in her husband's office."

Dana watched Greg's expression as he talked to Sheriff Brandson, attempting to determine whether he had received good news. But Greg's poker face revealed nothing. When he finally returned the phone to his pocket, he reported that a suspect had been taken into custody.

"Who?" they all shouted.

"An escaped convict from Arkansas, with a long list of priors. He's been in custody for several days, but Steve didn't say anything until they got the lab results back. He must have placed a rush order on them."

Dana asked what kind of prior arrests and was told they included kidnapping and sexual assault. "How did he escape from prison, Greg?"

"Steve didn't say but his DNA matches those found in the victims."

Dana shivered when she considered the murdered women. "Did he also kill Varina?"

"The Zagori woman wasn't raped."

"Then a woman must have killed her."

"Good possibility, but which one?"

It had to have been Camille Dressler. Darcun must have told the truth. Had they been wrong about him? Dana thought no. He was an ex-convict and couldn't be trusted. Sarah was staring at her, probably thinking similar thoughts.

"There's an all-points bulletin out for the Dresslers and the Gates. Jeff Dressler is apparently missing too."

Poor Josh. What will happen to the boy if he loses both parents? I'll adopt him and give him love and a good education. Dana wondered whether Walter would agree. She was no longer a single woman making decisions on her own. She had a husband to consider.

"Steve suggested that you remain in the motorhome until Varina's killer's arrested. There may be other residents missing as well. Deputies are canvassing the resort to determine that right now."

Sarah sat with Harry, holding hands, a frightened expression on her face. Dana wished someone were there to hold *her* hand. She must be getting old. The thrill of solving a murder case had dissipated like a lozenge on her tongue. All she wanted was the safeness of home and Walter's arms around her. She wished she could hear his reassuring voice, but didn't want to upset him by telling him about their current situation.

Someone knocked and Greg greeted an unseen visitor as though an old friend. "Be right back," he said as he closed the door. Dana could hear their muffled voices and assumed that a deputy had arrived. Had they discovered more suspects missing, or more bodies? And where was Darcun? She decided to boot up her computer to learn his first name. Two men had been listed in Rosie's profile. One of them had to be her son.

Scrolling through the list, she located Rosie and the names Alan and Marcus Darcun. So Marcus was Bob's real name. She turned to tell Sarah, but decided against it. The slightest mention of Darcun would upset Harry. The two of then seemed so happy that she decided to wait until later to tell them.

Greg reentered the RV scowling. "The Darcuns have

259

also disappeared."

Sarah rose from the couch. "But I just talked to Bob a few minutes ago."

Now was as good a time as any to break her own news. "His real name is Marcus Darcun," Dana said, "and we all know about his criminal record as well as his mother's. I wonder if Sheriff Brandson is aware of their backgrounds."

"I told him but he can't act on the information until he has proof that they were involved in the murder."

Sarah exhaled heavily. "So we sit here and wait."

"With me," Harry said smiling. "It'll give us a chance to get better acquainted."

Dana wondered if Harry were going to propose. She didn't think the time was right. When frightened, women usually made decisions they lived to regret.

Needing something to calm her, Dana set about making a batch of chocolate chip cookies— which Sarah usually made. When she had placed them in the oven, she decided to make a fresh pot of coffee. It would be a long night. Before the coffee perked, Sarah's cell phone rang and she rushed to retrieve it from the dining table. Checking the caller I.D. she said, "It's Bob."

Greg closed the gap between them, whispering, "Put him on speaker phone."

They all heard Darcun say, "Sarah, I can't talk long. My mother's holding me hostage."

"What? Where are you?"

"In an abandoned cabin several miles from the resort."

"Why didn't you call 911?"

"Because she's my mother and I don't want to get her in trouble. I think she's just popped her cork."

When Sarah looked pleadingly at Greg, he motioned for her to keep him talking. Rushing to the RV door, he stepped outside to call Steve. Dana knew they would attempt to trace the call.

"How could that tiny woman hold you hostage?" Sarah said, her voice heavy with skepticism.

"She insisted that I drive her here and handed me a document to read by lantern light. When I was seated, she hit me over the head again. When I came to, she had me tied to the chair. She threatened to shoot me if I told anyone that she killed Varina."

"Rosie killed Varina? But why?"

"Varina caused my dad to commit suicide."

Sarah held her thumb over the mouth piece when Dana gasped. "How do you know that, Bob?"

"Dad left a suicide note. He accused Varina of blackmailing him and draining his and mother's savings. He sold their house without telling her to pay Varina, so Mother was left with nothing more than his insurance policy and the motorhome."

Well, she's certainly not destitute. "Where's your mother now?"

"She went to the outhouse and will be back any second. She took the car keys but forgot about my cell phone. I managed to get my left hand free but the ropes are so tight I can't untie them."

They heard a woman shout and the connection go dead. Sarah repeatedly called his name but received no response.

"Do you believe him?" Dana asked.

Tears filled Sarah's eyes. "I don't know what to believe."

Dana said, "I wonder how that little woman killed Varina and managed to get her in the lake. She must have had help."

"Bob?" Sarah said. "Is that why he came to the resort? To help his mother kill Varina?"

Dana sighed. "If that's true, he's an accomplice to murder. But why would he tell *you* his mother's the killer?"

"Maybe to trick us into going there."

"He must know that we'd call the sheriff."

"Maybe he killed his mother and wants us to testify that she was holding him prisoner."

"We heard a woman yell at him, Sarah."

"But was it Rosie?"

Harry insisted that it was a hoax to get them there.

Greg opened the motorhome door, saying there wasn't time to trace the call. When they told him about Darcun's claims, he agreed with Harry. It had to be an attempt to lure Sarah and perhaps even Dana to a rural area.

"Where did he tell you to go?" Greg asked.

"He didn't. If it *was* a plot, Rosie screwed it up by yelling too soon," Sarah said.

Was his mother actually holding him prisoner? And why had he returned to the resort after he escaped her clutches? Because of Sarah? Dana reached for the coffee pot and managed to spill half its contents.

Sarah grabbed the phone when it rang again. Punching the speaker phone button, she motioned everyone to her side. Dana recognized the voice as that of Rosie Darcun.

"If you want to save my son's life, you'll come to the cabin alone. If the police arrive, I'll kill him."

"No, you won't. He's your only child and he helped you get rid of Varina's body."

Rosie's laugh was downright evil. "I told you it wouldn't work." She must have been talking to her son.

"Hand him the phone and we'll discuss this." Sarah glanced at Harry, who shook his head no.

A moment later, Darcun came on the line. "Are

you coming, Sarah? My crazy mother has a gun and is threatening to shoot me."

"So you want her to shoot me too?"

"No, of course not. She thinks I'm worthless and I need you to vouch for me."

"I can do that over the phone."

"She won't believe you unless you convince her in person."

"I have your number. I'll call you back." Clicking off, she turned to Greg, who said he would again call the sheriff.

They sat with Harry in the dining nook where Dana refilled their cups with the remaining coffee. Discussing past events, they concluded that Rosie was insane and her son an unwilling participant in Varina's murder. Harry wasn't so sure on the last point, but wondered how the disappearances of the Dresslers and Gates figured in. When Greg ended his call, he looked at Sarah expectantly, asking if she would willingly take part in a plan to trap the killer.

Harry objected but Sarah asked for details. Greg told her that she would be wired for sound and wear a protective vest under her clothing. Sarah smiled, remarking that she was already well padded so an extra layer wouldn't arouse suspicion.

"Are you sure you want to do this?" Dana asked when Greg had outlined the plan.

"As long as you and Harry are outside the cabin with your guns handy."

Greg said that several police snipers would hide within view of the cabin. They were experts at sneaking up on their prey. Dana and Harry could wait in a nearby van. Sarah nodded and picked up her cell phone. Checking the caller I.D. she punched in the numbers.

Darcun answered. "Sarah? Please come before this

crazy old lady kills me." His voice sounded on the verge of hysteria. Dana thought he must have taken acting lessons.

Taking a notepad and pen that Greg handed her, Sarah asked for directions. When she had written them down and repeated them back to Darcun, she asked to speak to Rosie. When she came on the line, Sarah told her she was coming alone but that she had to wait for Dana to return with the Jeep. It would take at least an hour to find the cabin in the dark.

"Don't tell anyone you're coming," Rosie warned, "'cause I'll be watching and I'll shoot this worthless son of mine if I notice anyone with you."

Chapter Twenty-Six

The police van met them on a secondary road nearly ten miles from the resort. Dana and Harry were told to wait in the van while Greg accompanied Sarah partway to the cabin. She had been fitted with the wire and vest while someone disabled the Jeep's interior lights. Sarah's hands trembled and she was afraid she would wreck the Jeep before she reached the cabin.

Greg went over her instructions again and told her not to worry. He and the deputies would crawl within a few feet of the cabin while listening to everything that was said. Sarah nodded and swallowed her regrets that she had allowed herself to participate. Greg's black outfit and watch cap, coupled with his blackened face made him nearly invisible as he sat beside her. The overcast sky had blanked out the moon. Gripping the steering wheel with both hands, she stared into the only light emitting from the headlamps.

Sarah was told to enter the cabin with a smile and Greg warned her not to antagonize either Darcun. He also told her to locate a place to take cover when they stormed the cabin. Shutting off the headlights she briefly stopped the Jeep so that Greg could leave undetected. She then proceeded on her own.

Remembering Varina's body floating in the lake, Sarah drove the Jeep as slowly as possible along the graveled road overgrown with weeds. The cabin had obviously not been used on a regular basis. Did the Darcuns suspect her collusion with police? The officers had quickly carried out their mission so as not to arouse suspicion. But would Rosie pat her down when she reached the cabin? Maybe Dana was right that Sarah had watched too many televised police shows.

The darkness crowded in. Tree limbs resembled masked men reaching out to grab a door handle. She stopped to make sure the doors were locked, then noticed movement off to her right in the undergrowth. Was it an animal or one of the Darcuns? Stepping down on the accelerator, she watched dust billow back into the headlights. A moment later a faint light appeared in the distance. It must be the cabin.

Can I do this? She thought of Dana and Harry back at the van, knowing they were frightened for her. She imagined Harry chewing the brim of his hat and Dana biting her nails.

Remembering the wire, she said, "Let's get this over with. I'm approaching the cabin and will let you know when I leave the Jeep... Dana and Harry, I love you both. I'll see you soon." *But will I?* Her heart pounded unevenly, her breathing more like gasps for air.

The jeep's headlights illuminated a small square of peeling log walls and weeds nearly as tall as Sarah's knees. A yard light showed her a place to park beside the cabin and no other car was in site. Perhaps there was a dilapidated garage somewhere in the area.

"I'm leaving the Jeep," she said without moving

her lips. "I hope you guys are here."

Stepping into the wind, she trudged around the cabin and felt a sharp jab in her back when she approached the battered wood door. Holding her breath, she waited. A woman laughed and told her to open the door and enter the unlighted room. The voice sounded like Rosie's with a slight lisp. Sarah stepped across the threshold and, remembering Bob's head injury, leaned against the wall.

When nothing was said, she asked, "Where's Bob?"

"If you mean my son Marcus, he's in the other room waiting for you. I'm surprised you actually came alone. Where's your friend?"

Sarah crossed her fingers. "At home. She told me not to come but I was worried about Bob— Marcus," she corrected herself.

"My son's a naughty boy. He lied about working for that magazine, and he didn't want to help me get rid of the body."

Sarah thought she had swallowed her tongue. Rosie was finally becoming visible in the dim light, but she couldn't tell whether the old woman was holding a gun.

"Why did you kill Varina?" Sarah's voice quivered.

"She bankrupted my foolish husband and me. I couldn't stand the thought of her doing the same thing to others, so I invited her to my patio and drugged her drink."

"How did you get her to come?"

"I told her my husband had left her a thick envelope, hoping she would think it was money."

"So you hit a golf ball into her head and did what with the body?

"I covered it with a tarp and hid it behind my overturned wheelbarrow until I could convince Marc to carry her to the lake. I knew he would. He always does what I ask. Eventually."

"Why are you telling me this, Rosie?"

"I'm terminally ill so I have nothing to lose. Except my son. He loves you and he'll need someone when I'm gone."

A frosty chill slid down Sarah's back. "Loves me? We don't know each other well enough—"

"And you love *him*. You just don't know it yet. That silly old fool Harry has whitewashed your brain."

"And if I don't love your son?"

"You'll join Varina in the lake. No one breaks my son's heart and gets away with it."

Sarah groaned, frantically searching for a way to change the subject. She then remembered Camille and the other missing residents. She asked if Rosie knew their whereabouts.

The old woman laughed. "I dropped by Camille's lot yesterday. She and Lacey were trying to decide whether to divorce their husbands. I told them to scare the hell out of them by taking them for a ride at gunpoint."

Shocked, Sarah asked if they had agreed to Rosie's suggestion. It could have landed them both in prison.

Rosie's laugh was more compassionate than before. "I think Camille was ready to shoot her husband and dump him in a swamp where the alligators would eat him. I've never seen a wife more scorned that she was. But Lacey wouldn't agree to that. She did go along with scaring them because Paul's in bad shape. She seemed to feel sorry for him. Maybe she thought he'd paid for his sin by suffering through the accident."

"Was it you or your son who cut the brake lines?"

Rosie moved closer and Sarah recognized a gun in her hand. "My brothers taught me mechanic skills while I was a young teenager. I can still crawl under a car and disable it. I punctured the line in the Jeep to discourage you and your friend from snooping."

"Then why did you cut Paul's brake line?"

"He asked some questions that made me wonder if he knew what I'd done."

"So you tried to kill him too?"

"No, just scare him."

Sarah caught a whiff of alcohol on Rosie's breath and knew that she had better end the conversation soon. What more would the sheriff want to know?

"Did you spray paint our motorhome, slash the tires and leave incriminating evidence in the storage compartment?"

That laugh again. "And a pretty damn good job of it, if you ask me. One of my husband's early businesses was locksmithing and he taught me the basics."

Sarah suddenly remembered the vest. She asked if Rosie had also killed the vest's owner.

"Certainly not," Rosie said indignantly. "I didn't kill anyone but Varina."

"Then how did you get your hands on the gray vest?"

Rosie hesitated before admitting to breaking into Liz's fifth wheel trailer when she learned of her death. "I know how much that vest meant to her and I was hoping she wasn't wearing it when she died. After I brought it home with me, I decided that it would be a nice touch to leave it with you."

Sarah inched further along the wall. "Was your son involved in any of your pranks?"

Rosie was so near she could have touched her. Waving her handgun, she said, "Of course not. My son is a putz. He's afraid of his own shadow and *he's* the reason you're here... You wouldn't have come if you didn't care about him."

Sarah slowly surveyed the room to locate a place to hide when the cavalry charged the cabin. But she was handicapped by night blindness. She would have to drop to the floor and hope for the best.

"Mother?" a familiar voice called. "Is Sarah here?"

Rosie moved forward to poke Sarah again in the ribs with her gun. "He wants to see you, Now."

Why weren't the police charging the cabin? Were they waiting for her son to confess?

Rosie switched on a flashlight that emitted erratic circles of light on the floor. The old woman poked Sarah again and they crept forward into another room. The cabin seemed devoid of furniture except for the chair where Bob was sitting. When the flashlight raised, she saw that he was actually tied, but she could see no blood on his head. She asked Rosie if she had struck her son's head again and was told no. It had been his idea to say he was wounded to elicit Sarah's sympathy.

"Such a baby," Rosie muttered.

"Sarah," he exclaimed. "I knew you'd come."

"Really, Bob? Why'd you drag me into your family dispute?"

"Because we're meant for each other."

Sarah bit her lip to prevent herself from denying his claim. She asked instead, "Did you help your mother kill Varina?"

"No, she did that on her own. I simply carried the body to the lake."

Varina drowned so Darcun had actually killed her, whether he realized it or not. What more did the police need? Had the wire malfunctioned? The silence was almost suffocating.

"Why did you leave her face up in the water?"

"I was an assistant to an ordained minister in my youth and I decided to baptize her before sending her on her way. Varina was beautiful and I wanted her to be found like a siren, not face down like a drowned rat."

Sarah realized her entire body was trembling. She had to get out of there. "I have a present for you in the Jeep," she said. "I'll be right back."

The old woman insisted on going along. Sarah prayed that someone would grab her gun the moment they left the cabin. The night air was even colder than when she had entered the cabin. And the night, as Harry would say, "was as dark as the inside of a boot." Could anyone see them?

Rosie's hand shook so badly that the flashlight's beam was unable to find the Jeep. Was her trigger finger equally unstable? Sarah pretended to stumble in the weeds and fall to the ground.

"Hold it right there," a man's voice said. Rosie screamed as she was grabbed, the gun discharging before it was wrenched from her hand.

Sarah heard another man's voice wail from inside the cabin. "Mother, come back and untie me."

Chapter Twenty-Seven

"Now that the murders are solved, the Darcuns in jail, and the Gates and Dresslers back home again, it's time to leave Paradise Acres."

Sarah sighed. "Harry wants me to meet his family. But I told him I couldn't let you drive to Wyoming alone."

"No problem. I've decided to trade in the motorhome here and take possession of a new one in Cheyenne. If you decide to go with Harry, I'll fly first to Sacramento to stay with Walter until after he leaves the hospital."

"I'll miss you, Dana. I don't know if this relationship with Harry will last, but I hope I've always got a home if it doesn't."

"You know you do. If it does work out, I hope you'll hold the wedding at the mansion. I'll fly Harry's relatives to Wyoming for the ceremony."

Sarah hugged her. "I wish you weren't quite so generous, my friend. Your inheritance is evaporating quicker than a cold tablet in water."

"Walter and I will have enough money to live on when he retires, especially now that we've decided not to investigate any more murders."

Sarah smiled. "I guess that means we won't be opening the Logan and Cafferty Detective Agency."

"I'm planning to write a book about our murder investigations instead."

"No one will believe what we've been through. They'll think a book titled *The Adventures of Dana Grayson and Sarah Clasbergan* is pure fiction."

About the Author

Jean Henry Mead is the author of 20 books, nine of them novels. She's also a national award-winning photojournalist, published domestically as well as abroad. She has written the Logan & Cafferty mystery/ suspense novels as well as Wyoming historicals based on actual events. Her Hamilton Kids' mysteries and nonfiction books are also examples of her work. Her website is www.jeanhenrymead.com and she can be found on a number of blog sites. The California native lives with her husband and Australian Shepherd on a ranch in Wyoming.